10/05

Wishing Moon

OTHER BOOKS BY MICHAEL O. TUNNELL

SCHOOL SPIRITS

BROTHERS IN VALOR:
A STORY OF RESISTANCE

Wishing Moon

MICHAEL O. TUNNELL

DUTTON CHILDREN'S BOOKS

New York

Library of Congress Cataloging-in-Publication Data

Tunnell, Michael O.
Wishing moon / Michael O. Tunnell—1st ed.
p. cm.
Summary: After a fourteen-year-old orphan named Aminah comes to possess a magic lamp, the wishes granted her by the genie inside allow her to alter her life by choosing prosperity, purpose, and romance.
ISBN: 0-525-47193-6
[1. Genies—Fiction. 2. Magic—Fiction. 3. Orphans—Fiction. 4. Middle East—History—Fiction.] I. Title.
PZ7.T825Wi 2004 [Fic]—dc22 2003062486

Published in the United States by Dutton Children's Books,
a division of Penguin Young Readers Group
345 Hudson Street, New York, New York 10014
www.penguin.com

Printed in USA • Designed by Tim Hall
First Edition
1 3 5 7 9 10 8 6 4 2

TO LLOYD ALEXANDER

Wishing Moon

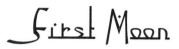

First Moon

· One ·

THE MOON MESMERIZED AMINAH. Standing in a gap atop the city wall, she stared at the cool, white disk rising above the desert.

She'd never seen a brighter night sky. The date palms surrounding Al-Kal'as threw out spindly shadows in the creamy light. The radiance caressed the rose-colored walls of Al-Kal'as, turning the stones the tint of a pink pearl.

"Maybe it's magic," said Aminah to herself. The Sultan's city looked different under this moon—beautiful, even civilized—but then she laughed, her voice cracking. "Or maybe I'm so hungry I'm seeing things."

To a visitor just passing through, Al-Kal'as appeared to be a prosperous place, but beneath the veneer of prosperity a second city existed—a city of misery. Aminah couldn't see the others like herself from her vantage point, but she knew they were there—hundreds, thousands who had been abandoned because they were blind, crippled, orphaned, widowed, or simply too old and useless. They were holed up in nooks and crannies, living in the streets on what they could steal or beg, barely surviving—or dying—in the shadow of plenty.

Far across the city rose the spires of the Sultan's palace. Its alabaster walls enclosed the source of Allah's Fountain, a miraculous torrent of fresh water that burst from the desert stone. After the first waters were siphoned off, the Sultan allowed the stream to continue in its path, giving birth and continued life to Al-Kal'as.

Turning back to the desert, Aminah breathed in the cool night air, scratching at the fleabites on her legs. Then, as she ran her fingers through her hair, capturing lice and squeezing them, she noticed movement in the street below and crawled forward for a better look.

Rina, again. Almost every night it was the same story, and the girl was only fourteen. *Like me,* Aminah thought, horrified yet fascinated.

The caravansary, where caravans came and went from Al-Kal'as, lay below. Nearby, there were several khans where travelers could get a room and something to eat. Men from the caravans, hungry for more than bread after their long journeys, had their choice of women—women who had no other way of staying alive.

The lunar glow glinted from the cheap bangles on Rina's wrists as a man led her into an alley. Her plump figure disappeared into the shadows.

She's eating like a princess, Aminah thought, her stomach grinding. *What I wouldn't do for a good meal. Perhaps . . .* Then she caught herself. *No! Never that,* she vowed. *One of these nights Rina will end up with a knife between her ribs.*

But hunger had already driven Aminah to break another promise she'd made to herself—never again to search for food in Beggars' Corridor. For the last week, every suq in the city had been packed with the Sultan's guards, and she'd been unable to steal the tiniest morsel from any marketplace stall. Aminah had had no other choice but to make her way to the Corridor.

Beggars' Corridor was an area on the outskirts of town walled off as a refuse heap. The garbage attracted not only rodents, but also what the Sultan's Grand Vizier called rats on two legs. Indeed, Aminah had witnessed beggars fighting rats for bits of gristle—or worse, preying on the rodents themselves.

But competition was stiffer in the Corridor than she remembered, and she spent most of her time running from danger. Her arms and back were laced with scars from knives, sticks, fingernails—even rats' teeth. For someone as weak as she was, venturing there was a death sentence.

As she crouched in her nest under the full moon, Aminah let herself remember living in simple comfort with her mother and father. Though her father, Omar, had not been paid much by the Sultan for his work, it had been enough. He had been one of dozens of scholars who toiled in the palace. He had studied maps and had read accounts of people from faraway places so the Sultan would know about the world— nations that posed a threat or might have valuable objects to trade.

Instead of living in the palace, as did many of the Sultan's advisers, Omar had chosen to keep an apartment in the city. It was small and far more humble than the Sultan's quarters, but he'd liked being away from the rigid formalities of the court and in the midst of busy city life. Living outside the palace walls had proved a sad mistake, however.

One morning on his way to work, his head in his maps and not on the street, Omar had been mowed down by a runaway horse and cart. He was dead in an instant.

The Grand Vizier cared nothing for the personal lives of the hundreds of servants, guards, and scholars who labored in the palace. Therefore, Aminah and her mother, Zaynab, were unknown to the Sultan's chief adviser. Had they lived within the royal compound, she and her mother may have had the chance to stay on as kitchen servants. It would have meant sustenance, at best. As it was, they were left to care for themselves in a city already filled with beggars. The one hundred copper carats that were left after Omar was buried were gone within a month, and Aminah was sent into the streets begging for food. Within six months, Zaynab was gone, too. Aminah was only twelve when her mother died, but she was old enough to understand that it was grief as much as hunger and sickness that had taken her. And she also understood that her mother hadn't cared enough about her own daughter to keep on living. When the body collectors finally found Zaynab, Aminah had abandoned her corpse.

A sudden rush of bitterness welled up inside, and Aminah turned angry eyes from the moon. "I won't give up!" she cried. "Not like she did." But Aminah knew she couldn't last much longer. She'd hardly had strength that night to climb the wall.

Her anger quickly changed to self-pity and tears. Why did she have to be alone? Everyone had abandoned her—even God. Though Aminah hadn't given Allah much thought in her young life, she still felt betrayed by Him. Couldn't He have spared one of her parents? As things were, she was haunted by hunger every moment she was awake and haunted by nightmares while she slept.

She missed her father most of all. Though often busy reading or lost in thought, he had made their lives safe and comfortable. He'd given them access to the palace. Now that life was an impossible dream.

In the midst of her misery, a thought struck Aminah with such force that she struggled to her feet. She stared at the moon, swiping at her eyes, and saw the image of a little girl from her past—the Sultan's only child. Her name was Badr al-Budur, the Full Moon of Full Moons.

Badr was only a few years older than Aminah. She remembered seeing her from a distance when she'd visited the palace with her father. Why hadn't she thought of her before now?

Aminah knew why. Since Zaynab's death, she had never lowered herself to beg, choosing instead to steal. She detested the idea of begging now, especially from the very people who had cast her aside like kitchen scraps.

Still, Aminah was desperate. It had never been this bad for her. Besides, the Sultan owed her something, she reasoned. After all, her father had been one of his men, so surely Badr would listen. *A woman's heart is soft,* Aminah thought. *She will help—if I can bear to ask.*

☾

PRINCESS BADR AL-BUDUR'S HAND PAUSED, her jade brush hanging above her long, dark tresses. She thought she'd heard a voice.

Badr cocked her head, but instead of catching sounds, she caught a glimpse of herself in the silver mirror she held and was distracted in an instant. *Such a lovely, shining face,* she thought. *I truly am the Full Moon of Full Moons.* The Princess smiled at herself with lunar radiance and continued brushing her hair.

There! She'd heard it clearly that time—the irritating whine of a beggar somewhere near her balcony. The Princess's bright face eclipsed into a dark scowl.

Al-Kal'as's riffraff didn't breach the outer wall often, though soon after she'd married her mysterious, wandering prince, the number of attempts had soared. The beggars acted as if they knew Aladdin personally, but of course that was impossible. Yet, Aladdin would treat them almost as friends, which angered the Princess. At Badr's request, her father had increased the guard, ordering them to be merciless. Aladdin wasn't to see or hear a beggar within the palace enclosure. Up until now, the guards had been so successful that Badr's bliss hadn't been disturbed in months, so the voice outside her balcony both surprised and infuriated her.

"Princess Badr al-Budur?" The voice was guarded but penetrating. It snaked into each of the outer apartments of the palace like a probe, searching out the Princess. "Full Moon of Full Moons?"

The Princess leapt to her feet, pillows scattering in every direction. Now the hoarse, desperate voice drifted up from directly below one of her many balconies.

"Fatimah!" cried Badr. "Fatimah, send for Saladin."

A round-eyed servant girl appeared in the doorway. "You called, oh radiant one?"

"Are you deaf? Fetch Saladin."

"The Captain of the Guard, oh effulgent one?"

Badr moved with startling speed, grabbing the girl by the throat. "Are you stupid, too? Yes, the Captain of the Guard."

She pushed Fatimah away. "Be quick—no, wait." Badr glanced toward the balcony. "Never mind. I'll take care of this myself."

The Princess waved the servant girl away and cast about the room for something to throw, something heavy but worthless. Her eye fell on the small chest in which Aladdin kept his battered brass lamp. Tarnished and dented, this bit of brass was the ugliest thing in the chamber. She'd never understood his attachment to such a piece of junk, when golden lamps encrusted with jewels lay about the palace like dust motes. But he would allow no one, not even the Princess, to touch it— much less fill it with oil.

"Aladdin values his garbage more than his wife," grumbled the Princess, as she snatched the lamp from its container and ran to the balcony. From her perch that overlooked the city, the Full Moon of Full Moons spied a girl, tall and thin and dressed in rags. She stood in the empty avenue that ran alongside the outer wall of the palace grounds.

The girl noticed Badr al-Budur standing on the balcony and, without blinking, returned her furious gaze. "Princess?" she asked.

The question set Badr's head spinning. How could the girl not recognize the Full Moon of Full Moons? Shocked into silence, she nodded.

The beggar girl smiled. "I'm glad I found you. My name is Aminah. You don't remember me, but I remember you, though I haven't seen you since I was a little girl. *My* father was a scholar in *your* father's court, but he is dead now. And so is my mother."

The Princess still couldn't find her voice. How dare a common street urchin look the Full Moon of Full Moons straight in the eye, much less speak to her?

Aminah chose to take the Princess's silence as a good sign—

perhaps of sympathy. "Understand, I'm not asking for alms. I can work in the palace," she said, unable to keep the stubborn pride from her voice, even though she knew no one in Al-Kal'as would think of hiring a young beggar girl. "My father taught me much. I can do sums. And I can write and read. And—"

"And nothing!" shouted the Princess, as she hurled the brass lamp. Her aim was true, and the lamp glanced off Aminah's brow with a sharp crack that echoed from the distant reaches of the deserted avenue.

The Full Moon of Full Moons smiled at the crumpled heap lying on the paving stones. "Thank me, Aminah, the scholar's daughter," she said. "I have saved your life by not calling the guards, though if I were you, I'd get up and out of here before they find you. Saladin and his men sling weapons more dangerous than rusty lamps."

☽

WHEN AMINAH REGAINED HER SENSES, she glanced up at the empty balcony. Her vision blurred, and she slipped back to the ground with a moan. Her eyelids fluttered, almost closed, when a flash of light pulled her back to consciousness.

The sun was about to settle behind the walls, and the avenue was crowded with shadows that crept forward like lurking rats. The lamp lay on the paving stones, and though discolored, it somehow caught the sunlight. With the slightest movement of her head, it flashed like a beacon.

Aminah crawled over to the lamp. She wrapped her fingers around the curved handle and picked it up. Cradling it like a baby, she stood on teetering legs and stumbled back the way she'd come.

She reached a point where the avenue branched into many alleys, a small city of warehouses and granaries. Earlier, the area had been bustling with workers, but the hour was late and the alleys were vacant.

Aminah leaned against the wall and looked back in the direction of the Princess's balcony, out of sight around a bend in the avenue. Now that her head had cleared a little, she was filled with bitter disappointment and bewilderment. She had hoped to find a soft heart and had instead found a stone.

Aminah lifted a hand to touch her aching forehead. Forgetting the lamp in her grasp, she rapped it against the bloody bruise and cried out in pain. Then she fell into hysterical laughter.

Feeling an odd sense of relief, Aminah turned her attention to the pitted piece of brass in her hands. It was worth a few copper carats at best, but that was better than nothing.

She felt the unnatural laughter building inside her again. "Why couldn't the Princess have flattened me with a golden bowl?" she asked, giggling. "Or a jeweled cup?"

The laughter died in her throat as the lamp grew warm in her grasp, and her eyes widened with pleasure. All at once, her stomach seemed gloriously full and her clothes clean and new. And, as if time had reversed itself, she was certain her mother and father were waiting in their apartment for her to return.

She drew back in amazement, and the lamp slipped from her fingers. Instantly, the vision of plenty was gone, and sharp pangs of hunger sliced her stomach.

As the lamp clattered across the paving stones, a harsh cry rose from somewhere in the empty streets. "Ahmad, do you hear? Over there! Near the granaries."

Fear pumped strength into Aminah. She leapt up, scooping the lamp into her arms. She ran, ducking into one of the alleys and narrowly missing Ahmad.

Aminah wriggled into a space between two buildings, only wide enough for her to inch along sideways. It was the entrance of a passage that led to an alley near the main suq.

Thin as she was, Aminah had to empty her lungs to squeeze into the opening. She'd just disappeared into the crevice when footsteps rattled past her hiding place. As the sound of the palace guards faded, Aminah greedily sucked in air. But fear, not breathing, and a rap on the head had taken their toll. She dropped the lamp and slipped down the wall as blackness engulfed her.

When she awoke, it was so dark that she wondered if she were awake at all. She couldn't remember where she was until she tried to move and found herself wedged between the walls. Her legs were splayed painfully to each side, and her face was smashed against the mud bricks. Somehow she found the strength to pull herself back to her feet.

She rested for a while, flexing her sore muscles, then started to sidle along the passage. Her foot knocked into something hard, and the object rattled against the wall. Aminah recognized the sound and smiled. She mustn't forget her lamp. It was all she had to show for risking her life.

She balanced on one leg, tipping over sideways to feel for the lamp. Her fingers found it, but she jerked away in surprise. It had tried to jump into her hand. Aminah leaned over again and found it waiting at the end of her reach. This time when she grasped the handle, the lamp stayed still.

Moving sideways like a crab, she edged along the passage-way. It was slow work made even slower because she was forced to rest every few steps. An hour later, Aminah slipped from the tunnel into a shadow-filled alley, relieved that no one was there to greet her. Though safe from the Full Moon of Full Moons and the palace guards, she was faint with hunger and bruised from top to bottom.

Too tired to travel back to her perch atop the wall, Aminah dragged herself into a murky recess in the alley—an old, aban-doned doorway. She wrapped up in her mother's worn shawl and pulled the lamp into its folds. As she tried to rest, Aminah remembered the warm sensation the lamp—it must have been the lamp—had sent through her body. And the happy vision of her old life. The brief moment of contentment made the ache in her heart seem all the greater.

She took out the lamp, holding it in front of her, but it remained cold to the touch. "If you are enchanted, your enchantments are cruel," Aminah murmured. "I'd be better off without them, so I'll sell you for a copper or two. And if I shine you a little, perhaps I'll get a bit more."

Aminah held the lamp in the crook of her arm, and with the hem of her shawl and a little sand that had blown into the cor-ner of the doorway, she began to rub at the tarnished brass. Once, twice . . . Then, on the third stroke, the lamp began to warm her fingertips. But instead of giving her visions, it began to shudder and hop in her grasp. It belched and erupted puffs of steam that shone with an eerie purple light. Aminah threw the lamp into the alley and pressed herself against the wall, too frightened and too spent to flee.

The lamp bounced and clattered against the stones, hissing and spewing clouds of glowing purple gases. It seemed to swell, and just when Aminah feared a terrific blast, the lamp stopped. It stopped shaking and spewing and rocked back and forth until it came to rest.

Then it exploded.

· Two ·

AMINAH THREW UP HER ARMS to shield herself from flying shards of brass, but she felt nothing.

"Say whatso thou wantest!" a deep voice thundered. "Thy slave is between thy hands!"

Aminah peeked through slitted eyes and cried out in terror. Standing before her was a fearsome man so wide his shoulders touched the walls on both sides of the alley and so tall he could peer above the buildings. He was wreathed in a throbbing purple light that made his bearded face and wicked scowl all the more terrifying. His burly arms lay crossed on his great chest, which was as broad and thick as an elephant. A golden hoop, large as a cart wheel, dangled from his earlobe, and a purple sash the size of a great tent girded his thick waist. Purple rays of light shot from a glowing amethyst ring circling one of his mighty fingers.

A jinni! Quaking, Aminah fell to her knees. She'd read about the jinn. They were spirits of great power—demons who could make a human's life miserable or snuff it out altogether. But on the other hand, Aminah also knew stories about jinn trapped in bottles or lamps who were doomed to serve a human master. A look of relief crossed her face as she remembered the jinni's words. He'd asked her to make a wish.

A wish! Relief erupted into incredulous joy, but Aminah fought the impulse to cry out in delight or even to smile.

"Say whatso thou wantest! Art thou deaf, girl? Answer me!"

The jinni's purple face ballooned until it was all she could see.

"I wantest thou to be quiet," said Aminah, her firm voice meant to mask her shaking knees. "All your exploding and yelling will bring the whole city."

The jinni looked surprised. His features faded to an ugly violet, and his head shrank like a leaking water skin. But he recovered in an instant, pumping deep purple back into himself.

"Be quiet?" he thundered. "No one tells me to be quiet. I may be trapped in this blasted lamp, having to take orders from every ninny who happens along, but I am no slave at heart. That lamp is all that stands between you and death, girl."

The jinni stuck out his chin and turned away. "How degrading," he grumbled to himself, and then he turned back to Aminah. "How insulting! Why, if I were a free jinni, you would not think of ordering me to be quiet. Do you imagine we jinn have no feelings? First you toss the lamp about as if it were a child's plaything. Do you imagine I found that pleasant? Then you insult me while I am about my work. Oh, this is just too much to bear. Why, I have a mind to—"

"Sorry!" shouted Aminah, desperate to make him stop.

His face lightened to a pleasing shade of lilac, and the demon grew smaller by half. "An apology," he said, seeming confused.

"Yes," said Aminah. "I didn't intend to hurt your feelings."

"Excellent manners for such a scrawny runt," said the jinni, leaning over to peer at her. "And a smelly one." The giant pinched his nose.

"Scrawny runt?" Aminah's eyes flashed. "Smelly? It's clear you know nothing about manners. How would you like it if I called you an overblown, loudmouthed bully? Or told you I think purple makes you look like an overgrown grape?"

"Over . . . overgrown grape?" said the jinni, sputtering. "Upstart! Unwashed lout!" His voice swelled to a roar, purple explosions erupting from his ears.

"I wish you'd settle down!" cried Aminah. "I've got palace guards after me. You'll draw them like flies to a carcass. Please be quiet!"

"Good enough," said the jinni. In the blink of an eye, the alley was still as a tomb. "All I wanted was a *please*. Was that so difficult? Besides, the noise was for you only. No one else could hear. Impress the master, but do not draw attention—one of the basic rules to which I adhere. Most of the time, at least."

"The rules! I wish to know all the rules," said Aminah.

"Rules?"

"How many wishes do I get? For what sorts of things may I wish? The wish-making rules."

The jinni stared at her.

"Oh, I see," said Aminah. "*Please, oh please*, tell me the rules."

The jinni scowled. "Whatso thou commandest. Thy slave—"

"Stop!" Aminah held up her hands. "Forget the 'whatsoes' and the 'thys.' Do you have a name?"

The jinni's purpleness vanished. His face took on a fleshy tone, and his eyes and beard were both the warm brown of sunbaked bricks. Though mauve gases still billowed from the lamp, encircling him with light, the jinni seemed less demon and more man. He uncrossed his arms and scratched his chin. His eyes took on a faraway look.

"A name. Yes, I once had a name." The jinni grasped at fleeting memories he couldn't snare, and then, with a morose expression, he turned to Aminah and shrugged. "I fear I have forgotten, so I think you should address me in this fashion." He bowed until his turban touched the ground and said, "Oh Noble and Magnificent Jinni of the Lamp."

Aminah laughed. "I'll shorten that to just plain *Jinni,* if you don't mind."

He shot upward until he towered above the alley again. He bared his teeth, which grew as sharp and long as swords, and then the top of his head erupted, spewing fire and ash. Aminah noticed with satisfaction that he accomplished all this without making the slightest noise.

"Oh, stop it," Aminah said. "You can't hurt me because I own the lamp. I'm the master, you're the . . . Well, never mind that. I'll call you Jinni and you call me . . . I know, you may call me Oh Extraordinary, Exalted, and Exquisite One."

The top of Jinni's head snuffed out, and he shrank to human size, a mixture of helplessness and disgust crisscrossing his face.

"I'm joking," she said. "I don't mind if you call me Aminah. That's my name."

"I will not," said the demon. "It is not proper. I shall only address you as Master or Mistress, unless you make a wish that I use your given name."

"How about *Miss?*" asked Aminah. "Will that work?"

"Yes, that is acceptable."

"Then call me *Miss,*" she said. "Now, Jinni, about those rules."

"As you command, Miss." Jinni swelled a tad and grew

faintly purple. "Between full moons you may make three wishes—three and no more. But with the rising of each full moon, you may begin again—as long as you possess the lamp."

"Three wishes a month," said Aminah, and Jinni nodded.

"Of course," he continued, "you may not wish for more wishes."

"Of course," said Aminah.

"And you may not wish that you will never lose the lamp to another. And you may not make wishes to cure the ills of all people, such as 'I wish everyone were happy and rich and kind.' We jinn cannot fix the world."

He paused, and Aminah thought he was finished. But then he said, "And you may not make wishes on behalf of the jinn."

"How's that?" she asked. "No wishes for you, Jinni?"

"No other human has asked to know the rules of wish making before beginning to make demands. You are the first to know this rule because you are the first to ask. Indeed, jinn cannot be the benefactors of wishes."

"Is it true that no one else has ever asked about the rules?"

"It is true," said Jinni, and his face darkened. "Greed made them all more demon than I. Even Aladdin—"

"It's *his* lamp!" said Aminah. "The Princess has no idea—"

"As I was saying," Jinni continued, throwing her a nasty look, "wish, wish, wish—until a rule was violated. Then the whining: 'What do you mean, no wishes left until the full moon?' Then the blaming: 'Why did you not tell me, demon scum?' Of course, no one ever thought to wish anything for me, so the rule never came up. Face it, I do all the work and get nothing for it."

"But what could a jinni possibly want? Or need?" asked Aminah. "You have such great power."

Jinni turned his back, and his voice was hard and low. "The power is yours, Miss, not mine. I have no life outside the lamp. I am not free."

"So it's freedom you want," said Aminah. "I doubt anyone would wish that for you, even if it were allowed. Why, if someone freed you, then he'd lose his own wishes. Who would do that, Jinni?"

"No human," he said, turning back to face her. Purple smoke billowed from his ears and mouth. "Now, Miss, you have learned the rules, and it grows late." He puffed himself up and his voice deepened. "Say whatso thou—"

"I thought I asked you to stop saying that."

"I will if you wish it. Is that how you would use your last wish?"

"Last wish!"

"You wished I would quieten, and if you have noticed, I have. You wished to know the rules of wish making, and now you do. So, one more wish until the moon is full again."

Aminah stamped her foot. "That's not fair!"

Jinni laughed. "Fair? You whine just like the others. And I thought for a moment you might be different, but you are no more than a selfish little child."

"Little child?" Aminah glared at him. "I've made it on my own so far. I don't need your magic. I don't trust your magic, come to think of it."

"Then you are also a *stupid* little child," said Jinni, yawning. "I will be going now, if you have no further need of me."

"Stupid!" Aminah cried. "I can match wits with the likes of

you any day! Why, I'm twice as—" She stopped, her face draining of its color. Hunger knifed her stomach, and her eyes blurred. She sank to her knees. "Perhaps you're right," she murmured. "Perhaps I'm being foolish."

"No question about that."

Aminah stared at Jinni. After a few silent moments, she nodded to herself and then spoke, her tone confident. "Give me a thousand gold coins, demon. Make it two thousand."

Jinni's smile was wide, though Aminah thought it had a cunning look. "To hear is to obey!"

In a puff of purple smoke, the demon vanished. Without his constant glow, the alley seemed darker than it had been before she'd rubbed the lamp. But soon Aminah's eyes adjusted, and she beheld hundreds of coins, tawny gold in the moonlight. They spilled from two large leather satchels onto the paving stones. The lamp, looking more dull and ordinary than usual, rested between the bags.

Aminah's eyes were locked on the gold, and she was unable to move. She had been tired and hungry and afraid for such a long time that her sudden change of fortune was beyond belief. At last, she staggered to her feet and edged toward the satchels, but instead of touching the coins, she bent to pick up the lamp. She rocked it in her arms, as the great, round moon pushed clear of the rooftops. Aminah laughed aloud and lifted the lamp to the sky. Then she touched the angry wound on her forehead. "Thank you, Full Moon of Full Moons," she said under her breath. "Thank you very, very much, oh witless one."

Setting the lamp aside, Aminah skipped and danced amid her treasure until a dark thought stopped her cold. Nothing was safe in Al-Kal'as. Even now a thief could be lurking in the shadows, waiting to slit her throat and steal the gold—and the lamp.

She cast nervous glances up and down the night-shrouded alley. She had to move the coins someplace safe and do it well before morning's first light. Merchants would be bringing their wares into the suq early. She thought of her perch on the city wall but knew she'd never be able to hoist so much gold so high before sunrise. Weak as she was, simply climbing the wall would be a challenge, even without the extra weight. *Perhaps I should have wished for food,* she thought. *Or better yet, a magic bag of food that would never be empty.*

Aminah couldn't think of another place to hide her treasure, except in the desert sands outside the city. If she buried the coins there, then in a day or two, when she had a place of her own, she could retrieve them.

She tied the lamp to her waist with a thin piece of rope kept handy in the pocket of her trousers, or sarwal, and made certain it was out of sight beneath her robe. Then she tried lifting one of the leather satchels.

With a startled grunt, Aminah collapsed to the paving stones. She may as well have tried lifting a full-grown camel.

For the first time, she looked closely at the coins. She expected dinars but instead found larger gold ducats, ancient and heavy. Not only were they heavier and more difficult to move than dinars, but they also were much more valuable and would be difficult to spend.

Aminah felt like weeping. She'd never be able to move this much weight. She pulled out the lamp and hissed into its spout. "You nas-s-sty, untrus-s-stworthy beas-s-st."

Wicked laughter rumbled from deep within.

Sighing, she set to work transporting the gold bit by bit. First, she emptied the satchels, then filled one of the bags with as much as she could carry. Back and forth to the doorway she went, until the ducats were out of the street, where a skulker might trip over them. For the rest of the night, Aminah lugged gold from the doorway through the shadows of Al-Kal'as, passing through a seldom-used portal that opened into the desert. Soon she was beyond fatigue and distress, going through the motions mechanically.

On her fourth return trip, Aminah stumbled into the alley and collapsed near the doorway. Making even one more trip seemed impossible, yet she would need at least another two. *Let someone have the rest,* she thought. *I can't go on.*

Suddenly a dark shape loomed above her, and a hand dropped with force on her shoulder. Aminah tried to scream, but her parched throat released little more than a whimper. The heavy hand swung at her face, missed its mark, then connected with her back and sent her sprawling. She covered her head against another blow as the figure raised his arm again. But instead of swinging, the man grew still for a moment, then began swaying wildly. Aminah rolled aside as his bulky form crashed to the pavement.

She stood on wobbly legs, ready to run, but the man—she could see his face now—lay unmoving. She smelled the reek of wine mixed with stale sweat and felt the bile rise in her throat.

The drunken lump let loose a juicy snore, and Aminah almost smiled. Fear still coursed through her veins, however, and with it she found new strength. Pushing the last of the ducats into the satchels, she was able to hoist twice the usual load and stagger through the narrow gate for the last time. She scratched a hole deep enough to accept the coins and, with the last of her energy, covered them.

When the sky lightened, the muezzins' cries breached the city wall.

> *Allahu akbar. Allahu akbar.*
> *La ilaha illa Allah.*

> *God is great. God is great.*
> *There is no god but God.*

Their musical chant stirred Al-Kal'as into wakefulness, but neither the muezzins nor the glaring sun stirred Aminah. She lay in a slumber as deep as death.

· Three ·

"YOU, THERE. WAKE UP!"

Aminah felt something sharp nudging her ribs. At the same moment, she felt the sun's heat burning her skin. Her tongue was swollen, her mouth parched, and inside her robe, she was dripping like a steamed vegetable. As she began to regain her senses, she recalled the startling events of the night before.

Her ducats! Aminah's eyes snapped open and took in two men dressed for desert travel. Kneeling over her was a third person, a much younger man—not far beyond boyhood. He was prodding her ribs with his finger.

"Good, she's alive," the young fellow said.

Aminah's eyes strayed past the men. Behind them was a string of camels—a caravan stopped on its way to Al-Kal'as.

"Perhaps she's deaf," said the tallest traveler.

Aminah continued to stare, dumbfounded, as the young man smiled at her. He had a pleasant face. Aminah felt the blood rise in her cheeks, and she tried to comb her hair with her fingertips. Then, realizing how filthy and ill-clad she appeared, she lowered her eyes.

"Here," he said, bending down and taking her hand. "Let me help you up."

Aminah attempted to answer, but her swollen tongue was stuck fast to the roof of her mouth. She felt a stab of fear mingled with wonder. In her experience, no one dressed like these men was given to pity for a shabby urchin. Though the young man's touch was gentle, she jerked her hand from his grasp and stared at the trio with defiant eyes.

"Perhaps she is both deaf *and* dumb, Hassan," said a small man draped in a colorful jubba. "Plus, she seems to possess the temperament of a camel."

Embarrassed, Aminah turned away, praying they would leave, and noticed the signs of digging where the ducats lay buried. She threw herself over the spot, spread-eagle.

"Oh no! The miserable little thing suffers from fits as well," the tall man said, with a frantic tug on his long, black beard.

"It's fortunate we noticed her," said the one named Hassan, "because she doesn't seem to have all her wits about her, either. No doubt lost and confused." He turned to the small man in the blue and yellow jubba. "Rashid, you have family in Al-Kal'as. Perhaps they'll recognize her."

Rashid snorted. "In a city this size? Besides, my people have moved from here. They wouldn't have mingled with this sort anyway—much less touched them." He stood aside as Hassan and the other traveler bent to lift Aminah.

She drew out what little spittle she had left in her mouth to loosen her tongue and cried out, "Get away! I'm neither lost nor witless. Mind your own affairs and leave me to mine!"

The three leapt back as if an angry scorpion had scuttled among them, not noticing the grimace on Aminah's face. When she'd thrown herself over the ducats, she'd landed on the lamp, hidden in the folds of her robe, and driven it into her back. She arched above it to relieve the stabbing pain.

"She speaks," Hassan whispered to the others, "but look! Her poor body is twisted and weak. How did she manage to wander so far?"

"No, no! You don't understand," said Aminah. She pushed the lamp to her side, keeping it concealed, and lay flat. "I had a cramp, that's all. I'm fine. That's why I'm here. On the hot sand."

The three cocked their heads, looking puzzled.

"The scorching sand helps my sore back." Aminah knew her story was beyond belief—plus, it was too early in the day for scorching sand—but she rattled on. "My family is poor. We can't afford a physician or even the hot baths to relieve my agony. So I use the desert for medicine. Now, please go. You're disturbing my treatment."

"Why, look there," said Rashid. "By the girl's right knee."

Everyone stared. To her horror, Aminah saw a gold ducat half-buried in the yellow sand. She was certain it wasn't a coin from her cache, but rather from the handfuls she'd stowed in the deep pockets of her trousers.

"No money for a physician?" asked Rashid, arching an eyebrow. "Either you're a thief or a liar. Or we've found hidden treasure. Move over, girl. Let's see if you cover more gold."

"Stop it, Rashid," said Hassan. "Your greed drips like the jaws of a starving jackal."

Rashid scowled but kept quiet.

Hassan turned to Aminah. "Is this coin yours?"

She tried glaring at him but found it impossible. His face was too beautiful. Instead, she lowered her eyes again, blushing. "I found it near the main gate of Al-Kal'as. It's enough money to feed my family for weeks, but go ahead, take it. I can't stop you."

"She stole it, as sure as the sun rises in the east," said Rashid, but the young man threw him such a dangerous look that he turned and stomped back to the caravan, the bearded traveler in tow.

Hassan pointed to the camels. "My father owns many such trains. He's given me responsibility for this one. So, I have no need to steal from you. The coin is yours. And I shall add a little to it. Gold ducats the likes of that one are rare, but perhaps I have a dinar or two."

Humiliation deepened the color in her cheeks. Aminah shook her head. "I don't want your money. And I don't need your help into the city."

Hassan released his purse, which seemed rather flat. "Fine. I respect your wishes, but you could be a bit nicer. I'm only trying to help."

She looked up at Hassan, gauging his sincerity. His honest, open expression only heightened the discomfort she felt over her tattered clothes and lice-ridden hair. Still, she couldn't make herself send him away. "What would help most is a drink of your water," she said.

Hassan lifted a water skin from his shoulder and handed it to her. She sipped at first, then took the water in great gulps. It seemed to nourish her, and strength flowed back into her limbs.

"Are you always so kind to beggar girls?" she asked, handing over the container.

Hassan pushed the water skin back into her hands. "Please keep it. My gift to you. Have you a name?"

She laughed. "Of course I have a name. Even beggar girls are given names."

Hassan looked hurt.

"Not that I'm a beggar, though I know I look like one." Her

face reddened again, and she hurried on. "Anyway, I'm sorry if I injured your feelings. My name is Aminah."

"Well then, Aminah, now that you've accepted my gift, you owe me the privilege of escorting you into the city."

"No! No . . . thank you. I . . . I still need the sand."

Hassan's brow wrinkled.

"I'll be fine. Please don't worry." She almost didn't recognize the warm sensation stirring inside her. It had been so long since anyone had been kind. She liked this boy. In spite of his wealth and station, he had a kind heart as well as a pretty face.

"Are you certain? I can find a physician for your back. And look, your forehead needs tending."

Aminah reached up to feel the wound and noticed her filthy, broken fingernails. She crossed her arms, hiding her hands. "It's nothing," she said, feeling awkward again. "I'll use some of your water to clean the scrape. Please, Hassan, you've done more for me than you can imagine. But I must stay."

Hassan sighed. "As you wish, Aminah." He reached out to touch her forehead, and this time she didn't pull away. "*Alsalamu alaykum,*" he said, then hurried back to the waiting caravan.

"Peace be with you, too," Aminah whispered.

· Four ·

HASSAN HAD BEEN Aminah's second bit of good fortune. Had he and his water skin not appeared, the desert sun might have baked Aminah like flat bread.

After Hassan and his caravan had moved on, Aminah smoothed the sand above the buried ducats. Noting the stone outcropping that marked her treasure's hiding place, she then returned to the city, gold coins clinking in the pockets of her sarwal.

By the time she slipped back through the small door in the city wall, Aminah knew how the rest of her day must go. First she would eat. Then she would purchase new clothes befitting a young woman of means. That way she would pass as the daughter, or perhaps the young wife, of a successful merchant. Then she would bathe before finding a place to stay.

But eating proved a problem. At a stall in a small suq, Aminah tried to buy dates with one of her ducats. The vendor raised an eyebrow and stared at her tattered clothing.

"I cannot change so great a sum," he said, fingering the coin. "Where did you come by a gold ducat? I hear the Sultan's guards have begun scouring Al-Kal'as for a beggar girl who stole a valuable trinket from the Princess. Might you have sold Badr al-Budur's bauble for this ancient piece of gold?"

Aminah grabbed the coin, her heart growing cold at the vendor's news. She hadn't given thought to the Princess's discovering the lamp's secret, but of course, Aladdin knew. He'd want his jinni back.

She edged away from the stall, unable to meet the merchant's eyes. "I do not steal," she lied, then turned and hurried down the street. She forced herself not to run.

The lamp bounced and clattered against her hip, feeling as prominent as a camel's hump. Aminah was certain the vendor would come dashing after her, even though he didn't seem to know it was a lamp the Princess had lost. She ducked into an alleyway, collapsing in a cold sweat. The merchant hadn't followed her.

Aladdin would undoubtedly offer a generous reward for his wife's "bauble." If word got out that he was searching for a brass lamp, and someone spotted the lamp-shaped lump under her robe . . .

Stop frightening yourself, Aminah thought. *No one will guess unless you panic and give yourself away.*

She stood and straightened herself, washing the bloody smear from her forehead and the dirt from her hands and face with Hassan's water. At least she could try looking like a servant rather than a beggar.

Aminah traveled the alleys until she found another suq. She came upon a larger shop, one that saw enough trade to change a ducat. This time she pretended to be on an errand for her master, explaining to the shopkeeper that her employer needed bread and dates right away, yet had no amount smaller than a ducat to send with her. Though the merchant grumbled a little, Aminah was soon away with food and smaller coins that would be easier to spend.

The bread and dates, washed down with the rest of Hassan's

water, left her feeling better than she had in weeks. With her confidence also fed, she decided to pick up some new clothes.

But as she neared the shop, Aminah realized she didn't know much about buying clothing. Her mother had always sewn her shifts and robes. She wasn't even certain what some garments were called. Feeling suddenly awkward, she lowered her eyes as she extended a tenuous hand to touch a plain, brown robe.

"Get away!" the merchant shouted, running from the back of his shop. "I won't have my wares soiled by your filthy little fingers. Paying customers may touch, but not the likes of you."

A flash of anger burned away her shyness. "I have money," she said, holding out a fist full of coins. "But I suppose it will go to someone less rude."

The merchant stared at her dinars. "Pardon me . . . Miss."

Aminah pointed to the brown robe. "I'll take that. And those . . . shoes. And that."

"The linen shift? A good choice—simple and comfortable."

"And that, too."

"What does a waif need with a lambskin money belt?" Without waiting for an answer, the merchant tossed the belt on top of her other selections.

Aminah glanced about, searching for undergarments, but didn't see any. Unable to muster the courage to ask, she had the merchant wrap her purchases, paid him, and then hurried out of sight, her face flaming.

She found an empty alley and hid until her cheeks cooled. She wouldn't be humiliated like that again, she vowed, and taking a bath was the first step. Then she'd find a shop where a woman could help her choose underclothing.

Aminah made her way to the public baths—the hammam. It was too early for the usual crowd of women, and so it was nearly empty. Though the attendants glanced at her with thinly veiled looks of disgust, they took her money and allowed her inside.

When she entered the steamy warmth, she felt she had wandered into a piece of heaven. Her muscles unknotted, making her drowsy. Her bruised body hadn't felt the comforting caress of bathwater for almost two years.

After soaking for a while, Aminah scrubbed until she was raw to get rid of the lice and fleas and then doused herself with scented oils. She hoped the attendants wouldn't notice the filth plastered on the tiles until she was well away from the bathhouse.

Afterward, she searched out another clothier, one of high reputation who would have no trouble accepting gold ducats. To her delight, Aminah was given over to the merchant's wife. Together they decided on sarwals and shirts of fine linen; robes and gowns of colorful, brocaded silk; leather sandals; wool coats; and delicate chemises and other undergarments that were soft as goose down against skin so long accustomed to rough rags. Aminah even chose an array of hijabs to cover her face. She had always hated the idea of women veiling themselves, but now she planned to use a hijab as a useful disguise.

As Aminah's selections began to mount, the clothier's wife began looking on in dismay. "Are you certain about that one, Miss?" she finally asked when Aminah chose an exquisite robe, a thawb with embroidery that must have required a dozen spools of gold thread. "It is as much as all the other things added together."

Aminah pulled several ducats from her money belt and dropped them into the woman's hand. Her husband, who'd come over to stop this girl from making fools of them, smiled so broadly that Aminah wondered if his face would crack. An hour later, when her shopping was done, the clothier was still smiling, but Aminah was not. She stared at the mountain of clothing, feeling the fool herself. What was she going to do with all of this?

"Take these leather traveling bags," said the beaming merchant, unknowingly coming to her rescue. "A gift, of course! We will pack everything for you and have the bags delivered. Simply give us directions to your home."

"I . . . I'm new in Al-Kal'as," Aminah stammered. "Bandits. Yes, bandits attacked our caravan. Took everything, except they didn't find the ducats. We buried them in the sand. Father was killed."

"You poor little sparrow!" cried the merchant's wife.

"Could . . . could you recommend a kahn—only the finest, of course," she said, warming to her lie. "I'll send word when my brother and I are settled. The doctors are still tending him, though his wounds weren't serious."

Draped in new finery, Aminah left the solemn couple, shaking their heads at her misfortune, and followed their directions to the inn. It was late in the day by the time she arrived at the kahn, but the innkeeper wouldn't give her a room.

"Disgraceful!" he blustered. "A young woman traveling alone. Unheard of!"

"I haven't a choice," she answered, and then told him the same story about the bandits, with a few embellishments.

"I'm alone, but I have some of my father's money. I'll pay in advance."

His face draped in a dark scowl, the innkeeper shook his head. "How do I know you aren't running away from your father—or worse yet, your husband?"

"Husband!"

"And where are your bags? Did the bandits steal them, too?"

Tired and frustrated, Aminah was close to tears. "My *father* is dead, and you would make life even more bitter."

"Relatives? Surely you have an uncle, a cousin?"

"Not in Al-Kal'as," she replied, hanging her head and stepping close to the man. She slipped a ducat into his palm.

The innkeeper glanced at the gold coin, his eyes widening. "Shameless, those bandits, taking a girl's father and leaving her with only the clothes on her back. Disgraceful! Come, little one, I have the perfect room for you."

To avoid drawing further attention, Aminah stayed in her room, paying a handsome sum to have her evening meal delivered and to have a message sent to the clothier asking him to bring her purchases to the kahn.

Aminah lingered over her food, rolling each bite over her tongue and sighing with pleasure. Hot roasted chicken stuffed with raisins and nuts. Buttered rice and steamed vegetables. Pancakes sweetened with honey. *This is a very fine kahn,* she thought.

Her shrunken stomach didn't allow Aminah to eat much of the feast but, unable to let the smallest scrap go to waste, she wrapped the remains in a towel and stowed them under the corner of her bed. Then she fell onto the mattress and pillows and was asleep in an instant.

Though the bed was luxuriantly comfortable after years of curling up in the streets, Aminah slept fitfully, plagued by bad dreams. The following morning, she awakened early, images of Beggars' Corridor and the Princess still swimming in her head. *Wealth will take some getting used to, I suppose,* she thought, blaming her rich dinner for bringing on the nightmares.

But Aminah couldn't shake off the unsettling effects of her dreams. She paced the room, driven by nervous energy, until she suddenly felt compelled to check on Badr. She decided to patrol the suq, listening for news about the palace's search for the lamp.

As she dressed for the day, Aminah couldn't resist donning the thawb embroidered with gold, sighing at its silky caress. However, she hesitated at the door when Badr al-Budur's angry features jumped into her head. She assumed the Princess wouldn't remember her face—one beggar looked like another to her kind. It was more likely, then, that Badr and Aladdin would have the Sultan's guard looking for a girl flaunting sudden wealth—an awkward, coarse girl accustomed to living on the streets. If that were true, she wondered if she dared stay in the kahn. The innkeeper would be quick to report a young woman passing out money like it was sand. And how stupid of her to part with so much gold at the clothier's and then have the packages delivered to her doorstep.

Now Aminah felt conspicuous in her expensive clothes, and she backed away from the door. She changed into the plain robe and linen shift she'd first purchased, securing the lamp beneath the robe's folds. "You'll be safe there," she said, patting the slight bulge at her hip.

She slipped from the inn unnoticed and wandered the suq, trying to think. How could she have set aside thoughts of the Princess, even for a few hours? Torn by indecision, she paid little attention to what was going on around her. *Should I find another kahn?* she wondered. *Or leave Al-Kal'as altogether?* She could take a caravan out of the city, but it was likely the Sultan's guards would be watching every departing traveler.

As Aminah sat down by the fountain in the center of the marketplace, movement at a brass merchant's stand caught her eye. She stood and stepped closer to watch several of the Sultan's guards sifting through the vendor's lamps. They were examining each one carefully, and she wondered how they were supposed to recognize the right lamp.

Before she could find out, a piercing scream brought her head around. More guards pushed through the suq, herding girls—beggar girls—toward the palace. The girl who had screamed now lay motionless on the paving stones. A guard hoisted her to his shoulder, and the somber troop continued on its way.

Shaking, Aminah slipped out of sight into an alley. She'd guessed wrong. Aladdin was rounding up every poor girl her age. Longing for her golden robe and a hijab to cover her face, Aminah followed side streets back to the kahn.

She stayed in her room for two days—staring out the window by night, napping uneasily by day, and eating almost nothing. Then she noticed that the innkeeper barely glanced at her anymore. Encouraged by his indifference, her anxiety began to ease.

On her fourth night in the kahn, a dwindling moon cast its soft light into Aminah's room, and she gazed into the star-speckled sky. She chided herself for being so timid. It was time to start enjoying her good fortune—to take advantage of her newfound wealth. After all, hadn't her father always admonished her to take hold of what life had to offer? To learn as much about the world as possible? She filled her lungs with the night air, sweet and clean, and imagined her old life slipping from her like a snake's skin.

The next morning Aminah ate a sumptuous breakfast, taking her time as never before to savor the textures and flavors of each morsel. Then she dressed in her finest new clothes and, veiling her face, set off for the marketplace.

As she neared the main suq, Aminah spotted two of the Sultan's guards nosing through the wares of yet another brass merchant. She forced herself to stand firm when her legs tried to take her in the opposite direction.

The vendor clutched his head, moaning as his lamps dinged against one another. Steeling herself, Aminah drew close enough to eavesdrop just as one of the guards threw down a lamp in disgust. "They're all beginning to look alike," he complained. "A tiny star engraved on the spout, says Captain Saladin. My eyes grow too bleary to spot it."

"Quiet!" his companion whispered. "Have you forgotten no one is to know what it is we seek? A loose tongue will cost your head."

Aminah caught herself reaching inside her thawb to look for the star and quickly withdrew her hand. The first guard looked her way, and his penetrating gaze chilled her.

The guard moved toward her. Perhaps bored with the

lamps, he only wanted to talk. But she didn't wait to find out. Spying a rough-looking boy crouched at the entrance of an alley, Aminah started toward him.

"There you are, Faris," she shouted, charging forward like an angry elephant. She grabbed the unsuspecting boy by the ear, though he was both older and taller than she, and pulled him to his feet. "I won't have you wandering away, leaving me alone in the suq. I have a good mind to have you dismissed, you lazy lout. Or better yet, I'll have Father beat you!"

Merchants and customers looked up in surprise. A merry tune coming from a small group of street musicians fell into sudden disarray, the sounds of horns and lutes and drums trailing into silence. Everyone in the suq stared at Aminah.

The boy was too surprised to react. Before he was able to cry out or run for his life, Aminah looked him in the eye and winked. His eyes strayed beyond her shoulder to the guard, who had pulled up, grinning, to watch a poor servant's misfortune. Then the boy fell to his knees.

He let loose a piteous howl and threw himself, facedown, at Aminah's feet. "No, Miss! My poor mother will starve. My sister will die without money for medicine. Please do not dismiss me! Have me beaten. Beat me yourself." He looked up long enough to spot a large crooked stick lying close by, then scrambled to get it.

"Here," wailed the boy, handing Aminah the stick. He turned his back to her. "Strike me, Miss! I deserve it—and worse. Whack my poor, miserable spine! Slap my tender but worthless skull! Please, Miss. I shall be forever grateful for the lesson."

"Lay it to the wretched little whelp!" someone yelled.

"She's too skinny to hurt a fly!" cried another voice. "Here, let me do it for you."

The band of musicians began playing a sad, heavy melody to accompany the unfolding drama.

Aminah stood, dumbfounded. She stared at the stick in her hand and then tossed it aside. A disappointed groan rose from the suq, and the crowd turned back to its business. The guard shook his head in disgust and moved back to the lamps.

"I'll forgive you one last time, Nasir," Aminah said in a loud voice.

"Faris," hissed the boy.

"Only one more time, Faris, *son* of Nasir! Now, come along!"

The boy trailed behind Aminah until they were well away from the suq and the palace guards. When they were alone, she fell against a wall, taking a deep, shuddering breath.

The boy dropped to the ground, laughing. "Hit me harder, Miss. Hit me harder!" he cried.

"Well, thank you, Nasir or Faris or whoever you are," said Aminah. "But you were almost too good an actor. If you'd carried on much longer, the guards would have smelled a rat."

Rising to his knees, the boy bowed, his head touching the pavement. "I am called Idris, Miss. And I never go too far with my acting—always just far enough. I don't know why you fear the Sultan's men, and I don't want to know. I only hope my services may have been worth something to you."

"Yes, I suppose I owe you something," she said, turning away to reach into her money belt. "Here." She dropped some coins into his outstretched hand.

"Five dinars!" Idris grinned. "Very generous, Miss, but is it enough for saving your life?"

Aminah shook her head, surprised. "Saving my life! Who said anything about saving my life? But I suppose your brilliant performance might be worth two extra dinars." She laughed, tossing him the coins. "It must have been a shock, my grabbing your ear. It was quick thinking to play along. Thank you."

Idris sighed. "A young woman of your obvious wealth needn't be so tight with her money."

"Why, you ungrateful—" Aminah threw three more coins onto the pavement and turned to leave.

"I'm sorry, Miss. Wait! What is your name?"

Aminah hesitated. "It's . . . Zaynab," she answered over her shoulder. Her mother's name was the first to enter her mind—given more time, she would have chosen another.

"An honor to meet you, Miss Zaynab. And you are quite right—you have overpaid me. I feel I owe you something more. So ask what thy will, Zaynab the Magnificent. Thy slave is between thy hands!"

Her eyes grew wide at the jinni's words. Did this boy know about the lamp? No, Aminah quickly decided, that was impossible. "You've been listening to too many stories, Idris," she said.

He shrugged. "A good story is worth more than gold," Idris said. "I'd return all these dinars to know yours. Well, perhaps half the dinars. Those fancy clothes hide a girl who's in trouble. I think you need my help."

"Need help?" Aminah turned back to him. "I don't need help—from you or anyone else."

The boy studied her face. "Was it my imagination, or was that you who needed my help a few minutes ago?"

Aminah's eyes flashed. "Good-bye, Idris."

His arm lashed out, and he grabbed her hand. Before she could react—scratch or kick or cry out—he released her and quickly strode from the alley. Moments later, Idris had disappeared into the suq's dense traffic.

Aminah looked down. Five dinars lay in her palm.

)

THAT NIGHT in her room, Aminah puzzled over what had happened with Idris. She'd thought him a ruffian, but he had turned out to be . . . She wasn't really certain what Idris had turned out to be, except that he was more of a gentleman than she had expected. And he seemed to possess a talent for acting.

She shook her head and tried to sleep. Instead, she lay gazing at the ceiling, wondering what it would be like to be his friend, even if he were only playing the part. It would be so nice to have someone to talk to . . . But one lesson she'd learned from two years of living in the streets was that she could never trust anyone. The secret of the lamp suddenly seemed a burden larger than she could bear—especially by herself. That thought filled her with a crushing sense of loneliness.

Aminah felt as abandoned as ever. Allah had blessed her with riches, but it was a poor substitute for a family—and for her liberty. At least as an urchin she'd been free to roam the city. Now she was a prisoner of the kahn, hiding from Aladdin and his princess.

Could my wish have brought me less satisfaction? she thought.

· Five ·

RESTLESS AFTER ANOTHER DAY of hiding in her room, Aminah pulled herself from the kahn. She knew she couldn't stay there much longer but had no idea where to go. She wandered aimlessly, trying to decide what to do—until she was brought up short by the sound of horses. Drawing nearer the neighing and pawing, Aminah rounded a corner and stepped into a great open space.

The place was a sea of horses, and Aminah's spirits lifted at the sight of them. She'd dreamed of horses when she was little but had never yet ridden one.

Maybe it's time, she told herself, and then was struck with a daring thought. This could be her way of escape! She'd ride into the desert at night, and if she were lucky, no one would notice. She'd head for Baghdad or Tyre or one of the many places her father had dreamed of visiting.

Energized by her plan, Aminah hurried toward a horse trader with a line of handsome Arabian stallions tethered to a long rope. The man ignored her, continuing to groom one of the horses. She turned to slink away when another of the stallions nuzzled her shoulder. Through her veils, she felt its warm breath against her neck, and her resolve stiffened. She cleared her throat to get the trader's attention. "I'd like this horse," she said.

He glanced at her and turned back to his work.

"I would like to buy this gray horse," she repeated, more loudly.

The man's sun-blackened face wrinkled with irritation, but he turned to her. "I do not deal with women." He spat into the dirt, churned by sharp hooves. "What are you doing here alone? It is not seemly for a young woman of your means. I have a mind to ask the Sultan's guards to escort you home—at least away from this place."

"Pardon me, sir, but she is not alone."

Aminah whirled around to face Idris. He seemed a little cleaner—even a little taller—than yesterday.

"I am her father's servant. He sent me to accompany his daughter on this venture. Forgive me, Miss Zaynab, but my eye was on a horse across the way. I think it is one you will fancy."

"And what would the likes of you know of horses?" the trader said scornfully.

Idris drew himself up. "I have spent my whole life in my master's stable."

The man laughed. "It matters not, boy. I will be happy to take your master's money."

"And you may get the chance," said Aminah, raising her chin. "But first I will see what Idris has to show me."

"You'll find no better than what you see here," the man said, but Idris ushered her away.

When they were out of the horse trader's line of sight, Aminah reached for a dinar and held it out to Idris. A scornful look crossed his face. With a disgusted sigh, she gave him three.

"You don't know a thing about horses, do you?" she said.

"Of course I know horses," he answered. "I was nursed by a mare and schooled by a stallion. When I ride, it's as though I'm part of the horse."

"The rear-end part, I'd guess," said Aminah.

Idris laughed. "Maybe you're right."

He walked away from her toward another line of horses. She was surprised to find herself following him.

"Now, this is the mount I'd buy," Idris said, as she approached. He rubbed the neck of a regal, russet-colored stallion. Aminah noticed the look of love in the boy's eyes. "But I'd wager you've never touched a horse, much less ridden one," he continued. "So why were you after the gray fellow over there?"

"You don't know me any more than I know you," Aminah retorted. "Stay out of my business."

Idris held up his hands. "I'm only trying to help. I must say, you're making it hard for a newcomer to feel welcome."

"Are you telling me you're not from Al-Kal'as? Is this another of your tales?"

"I've only been here a few days. I came with a caravan. I worked for a horse trader who was bringing mounts to Al-Kal'as. But we were raided not far from here, and he was killed. We lost all the horses, too. I'm lucky to be alive, I suppose."

"You don't seem too upset by your poor master's misfortune," said Aminah skeptically. His story was almost identical to the one she'd invented the other day. "Why should I believe you?"

"Would I lie to such a fine lady?" he said, with a smile.

"Without a second thought," she said. "Why are you following me? What do you want?"

Idris clutched his heart. "I am injured by your words, Miss Zaynab. I want nothing but to erase the worry from your pretty brow."

"Will that be one dinar or two?"

Idris looked puzzled.

"For the compliment. Don't tell me you charge more than two!"

"I believe I've met my match," said Idris, grinning. "Let me be honest. I need your money, but I will not steal it from you. I'll be your bodyguard—your servant. You're mysterious, Zaynab—mysterious and in trouble. We can help each other."

"Bodyguard? You've the brawn of a withered corpse. I'd fear for my life every minute," said Aminah. "Besides, I'm not in trouble."

"As a troublemaker, I pride myself in recognizing trouble; and you, Zaynab the Magnificent, are in trouble. You look rich, but where do you live? Where is your family? Why do you fear the Sultan's guards? I'm guessing you wanted that horse to escape Al-Kal'as because the guards are watching the caravans. But you'd never survive the desert. If the bandits didn't get you, the sun would."

Aminah fidgeted, embarrassed that Idris had seen through her and she'd been stupid enough to think she could cross the desert alone.

"Let me be your friend-for-hire," he said. "I can be quite loyal."

Aminah leveled cool eyes at Idris, examining his face for signs of treachery. She saw none, but then he was a very good actor. "Loyalty has nothing to do with money," she said.

"Well, there is the fact that I like you," said Idris. "You remind me a little of someone."

"Who?"

He shrugged. "It doesn't matter."

"Who?" she asked again.

He thought for a moment and then said, "I once had a sister—Saffiyah. She was headstrong—like you."

"Headstrong!" Aminah cried, then grew quiet. "Had?"

Idris nodded. "You even look a little alike. So, what do you say? Am I your new friend?"

Aminah's heart thumped against her ribs, even though she already knew she was going to chance it. She didn't believe a word he had said about his sister, but something inside told her Idris wasn't dangerous.

Life is a steep mountain for a lone woman to climb, she thought, a sour taste in her mouth. *Perhaps Idris can level the path.*

Yes, he might be useful, and so she would buy his friendship—for now.

ﭢ

AMINAH DECIDED that the most important thing Idris could do for her was help her buy a place to live, to get her out of the kahn. Just as he'd made it possible to deal with the horse trader, he could give her access to a merchant of properties without raising suspicions. The first step was to get him to the hammam, and then to dress him like the young manservant of a wealthy merchant's daughter.

"I clean up nicely, don't you think?" asked Idris, as they left the clothier later that day. He stroked his silk shirt with genuine pleasure.

Next Aminah gave him money to rent a room in the same kahn where she was staying. As she handed over the coins, she marveled once again that she'd let him into her life at all. It was unnerving, as was being called by her mother's name.

"I didn't tell you my real name," Aminah finally admitted. She'd smuggled him into her room for a conference, but not before carefully hiding the lamp.

"I suspected as much," Idris answered. "However, you may trust that my name is, indeed, Idris."

"And I'm Zubaydah," she said, without blinking. It was the name of her father's only sister. She, too, was dead, but Aminah harbored fond memories of her.

"It's a pretty name," he said.

Aminah wondered if there was a disbelieving tone in his voice, but she decided it was her imagination. Still, she hurried to change the subject.

"I have a plan. We'll dress you up as an Abyssinian eunuch. That way, no one will question my having such a young manservant following me around. It's good you don't have a beard yet, since they don't have whiskers. I'll darken your face with dye, and you can wear some padding. Every eunuch I've seen is heavy about the hips. Something to do with losing their manliness, I think."

"Are you insane?" Idris stomped about the room. "You don't possess enough gold to make me dress up like one of those . . . those—why, they're not even men. Being whiskerless at my age is bad enough. I'm not padding my hips. Or dyeing my face."

"Fine," said Aminah. "I guess you really didn't mean it."

"Mean what?"

"That you wanted to help me."

Idris raised his eyes to the ceiling.

"New clothes and a room in the finest kahn in Al-Kal'as," said Aminah. "And this is how you show your thanks. I suppose I'll just have to find someone else."

Idris snorted. "Good luck!"

They stared at one another with fierce determination. Finally, Aminah sighed. "It's an act, Idris. You're an actor. I thought you'd like doing this."

Idris shook his head violently. "Are you trying to kill me? I'll die from the heat, draped in all that padding. Here, take back the clothes." He stripped off his robe and threw it at her feet. "They're not worth what you're charging me."

"You win," she said, throwing up her hands. "No eunuch disguise."

Idris grinned. "Good! But the padding doesn't have to go to waste. You could stand using a little of it yourself."

Aminah looked down at her chest. Loose clothing helped to hide her underdeveloped body, but she had to admit a more rounded form would make it easier to masquerade as someone older and more independent. Still, Idris had no business pointing it out.

"You're a beast," she cried, but Idris was laughing as he rubbed his chin with exaggerated strokes.

"No whiskers, eh? A baby face, you say? Well, then, an eye for an eye, a tooth for a tooth, an insult for insult," said Idris.

"Get out of here," Aminah said, fighting a smile.

☽

THAT NIGHT, when the kahn was at rest, Aminah wrapped herself in a black robe and crept into the streets. She passed through the city wall and into the desert, taking every precaution that no one, including Idris, would follow her. Pacing away from the stone outcropping, she found the ducats' hiding place, filled her money belt and the pockets of her sarwal, and was back at the inn before anyone had stirred.

Later that morning, Aminah met up with Idris, who put on a humble face and walked behind her at a respectful distance. His presence seemed to protect her from clicking tongues and questioning glances and, as she suspected, having him along made dealing with the merchant of properties an easy matter.

"My mother is dead," she told the merchant, repeating the story Idris had helped her concoct. "And I am an only child, much to my father's sorrow. No sons to handle his affairs when he is away. And he is away most of the time."

"It must be a terrible burden," he said, shaking his head sadly. "What does your esteemed father do, to take him away from Al-Kal'as? And does he not have a manservant who could do this work for him?"

"My apologies, but he forbids me to speak of his business affairs. Except for the purpose of my errand." Aminah ducked her head, as if she were blushing. "He wants to purchase a dwelling to use as part of my dowry."

"Oh my!" the merchant exclaimed. "He must be very rich—er, must love you very much. Such a magnificent dowry! Funny, I don't recall hearing of Malik al-Ashtar. And I know most wealthy men in the city."

Aminah shrugged. "Please, forgive him for sending me. At least he did not send me alone."

Scowling, Idris straightened to his full height. His stern features and splendid clothing made him look older. At the same time, Aminah opened her belt and pulled forth a handful of ducats. The merchant's greedy eyes swelled, and he stopped asking questions. She noticed that Idris's eyes swelled, too.

Before the day was done, Aminah found the perfect place on the fringes of Al-Kal'as, near the Sultan's olive groves. Surrounded by a wall, the house was built of kiln-baked bricks and was big enough to house a large family in rich comfort. Its beautiful gardens were ladened with the springtime scent of jasmine, which drifted into every room, and a fountain burbled in the center of its courtyard. From the rooftop terrace, Aminah surveyed the estate with pleasure.

"Here are fifty gold ducats toward the price," Aminah said to the merchant of properties, emptying her belt and pockets. "Father requests that this be the portion of my dowry that will remain my property, in case of divorce. Place ownership in my name. I am Zubaydah."

The merchant nodded, trying not to look surprised as he counted the gold coins. "I haven't seen ducats such as these in years—at least not so many together." He turned one of them over and over, a look of love softening his face, then finished counting. He looked up, concern etched on his brow. "There are only forty-four, Miss."

Aminah leaned forward, starting to count them herself, but Idris dropped six ducats on the table. "You have a hole in your pocket," he said.

"You are fortunate I have a better sense of humor than my father," Aminah said to Idris through clenched teeth. She turned to the merchant. "My servant and I will deliver the remainder to you tomorrow. Prepare the necessary papers."

On the way back to the kahn, Aminah frowned at Idris

over her shoulder. "Why didn't you tell me earlier?" she asked tartly.

"I had something to prove," said Idris.

"That you're a thief who changed his mind at the last second?"

"No, that I could have taken the coins without you knowing—but I didn't."

"I wish I could be certain of that."

"I am not without honor!" The outrage in Idris's voice sliced through her, leaving her breathless. "I promised not to steal."

Aminah nodded as if she believed him, but she wasn't at all sure. *He could be lying,* she thought. *Maybe he knows about the lamp, and this is part of his plan to take it for himself.*

"Perhaps you'd better go to the merchant alone next time," he said, his icy tone revealing that he sensed her doubt.

"No," Aminah answered. "I need your help."

They walked the remainder of the distance in silence.

❭

BY MORNING, Aminah had a box loaded with the gold and waiting for Idris. She wanted to send him alone—to test him, to test herself—but she didn't dare. So the same two-person procession made its way to the merchant of properties.

Aminah slept in the new house that night, though it was bare. She had picked up a few cushions and blankets in the suq—enough to make up two beds, for she'd decided to allow Idris to stay. She put him in a one-room outbuilding that had once housed the gardener. *To keep him as far away from the lamp as possible,* she told herself.

It seemed to Aminah that Idris had accepted the weak apology she'd finally managed to offer. He'd been happy enough with his accommodations and had shared their evening meal of dates and cheese as though it were a feast. Afterward, when she'd locked her doors and settled among the cushions, Aminah admitted to herself just how much of a blessing it was to have Idris on the grounds—and yet that blessing warranted close watching.

· Six ·

BEFORE A WEEK WAS OUT, Aminah had retrieved the remainder of the treasure—without Idris's help. She stole into the desert each night and was always back in time to be rested and waiting for Idris to report for work duty. She insisted he earn his keep, and to her surprise, he didn't seem to mind laboring to restore the gardens, replacing missing roof tiles, or scrubbing down the kitchen. His willingness made her even more suspicious of him. *No one would be this helpful without a hidden purpose,* she thought.

As the days went by, Aminah noticed that the lamp had left a scar in the middle of her forehead—a strange purple mark shaped like the small star engraved on the lamp's spout. Every time she looked in a mirror, the star reminded her she was being hunted. This reality seemed to color all of her actions and decisions.

Aminah had purchased the house using her aunt's name, hoping that Badr would never connect Zubaydah to the beggar girl who stood below her balcony. Idris didn't know her as Aminah, so it was impossible for her name to slip from his tongue. She even regretted telling that traveler, Hassan, her name, though he must be far from Al-Kal'as by now.

As safety was on her mind, Aminah was particularly pleased with one feature of her new house that Idris did not know about. In her quarters, some ingenious craftsman had cleverly concealed a small room behind a sliding panel carved from sandalwood. The panel hid an iron door that could be opened only by turning three small wheels on its surface. By aligning the proper combination of symbols on the wheels, Aminah could enter the room. Inside, she placed the rest of the gold ducats, the lamp, and Hassan's water skin. Only then did she feel free to leave the house without taking the lamp along.

After her last trip from the desert, Aminah was dismayed to find that the ducats filled only one small shelf in their new hiding place. Had she spent so many? With shaking hands, she began counting the coins, then tossed them aside with a laugh. Jinni could fill the room if she commanded—which was exactly what she would do.

"I'll never be poor again," she said aloud, surprised that it had taken her so long to comprehend this fully. Then another thought made her grin. With Jinni's magic, she should be able to avoid Aladdin and Badr. *Perhaps I'll wish for the power to fly,* she thought, suddenly giddy with the prospect. *They'll never catch me then. I could fly away from Al-Kal'as for good.*

"Aren't you looking bold today," Idris said the next morning. He'd noticed a new, confident swagger in Aminah's step.

"Follow me," she said, enjoying the commanding tone in her voice. "We're off to the suq. I need some things for the house."

"Are we . . . you getting carpets, diwans—perhaps other furnishings?" Idris asked. "It's about time we . . . you bought some. And hot food would be nice, for a change. I'm not complaining—dates and bread and cheese are tasty enough. Just curious, that's all."

"Can you cook?" asked Aminah.

"Cook! Are you joking?"

"Well, neither can I," said Aminah.

"Didn't your mother teach you anything?"

Aminah flinched at the mention of her mother. She turned on Idris. "You're the servant here."

"I just thought . . ."

"Yes, yes, you're right," she grumbled. "I should know how, but I don't." Why hadn't she been taught, like every other normal girl? Had her mother thought her incapable?

"Cheese and dates, then," said Idris.

Aminah sighed. "I'm willing to try my hand at cooking—if you'll help."

"Why not," he answered with a grin. "Even though it might be fatal."

When they reached the suq, Aminah was surprised to discover that Idris had a sharp eye for quality—both in furnishings and food—and let him make most of the purchases.

"Who *are* you?" she asked, after watching him analyze carpets for tightness of weave, quality of wool, and permanence of color. "No stableboy would have such knowledge— and fine taste. I hear a good thief knows what's shoddy and what's not."

"I'm simply more civilized, much more cultured than you," he said. "Watch and learn, waif."

"I'm serious. Where did you come by this?"

Idris stopped, turning to Aminah. "Unlike you, I will reveal my background. Before my journey to Al-Kal'as, I really was a stableboy. But I was so good with the horses that my master began taking me along on his business trips. Yes, he bought and sold horses, but he traded in everything else. He knew the ins and outs of precious gems, fine brass, excellent carpets—almost anything you can imagine. I watched and listened and learned."

Aminah nodded, impressed. Though she didn't trust him, she found Idris endlessly fascinating. "Lead on," she said. "We have a kitchen to equip."

By day's end, they had filled Aminah's house with the best of everything: rugs and tapestries woven by master craftsmen, imported furnishings, the finest copper bowls and pots. She did not worry about attracting Aladdin's attention because Idris was doing the shopping—not the skinny girl Badr had struck with the lamp.

They had also filled the larder with fine white bread; rice and rich butter to douse it in; sweetmeats dripping with honey and covered with almonds; mounds of melons, pomegranates, and dates; various flavors of sherbet—banana, lime, orange, violet, mulberry—to quench their thirst; spices of every sort. But they both were too tired to try their hand at cooking and once again settled for dates, bread, and cheese. Tomorrow, Aminah decided, they'd buy a chicken for roasting or perhaps some fish to be fried in vinegar and sesame oil (Idris remembered such a dish from his old master's table). However, they enjoyed sweetmeats and melon and washed everything down with sherbet cooled by shavings of ice.

The ice had cost a king's ransom when compared to the price of a chicken, but Aminah sighed as she sipped from her glass and said, "Worth every dinar."

"Having ice for the first time was . . . well, I suppose it was wonderful," said Idris. "But extravagant, don't you think?"

"You didn't worry about extravagance when we were buying carpets and copper pots," Aminah answered. "Why worry about a few shards of ice?"

"Because this thought just came to me: what if Zubaydah runs out of ducats? It's not as if you have a way of earning more—or do you?"

His blatant question left her choking on her drink. "If you're so concerned," Aminah asked when she recovered, "why don't you find work?"

"Work!" Idris laughed. "Taking care of you is a full-time job. Besides, in a city filled with beggars, where would I find work?"

"I believe I'm the one taking care of you," she said indignantly.

"A poor choice of words," said Idris. "Of course, I meant to say *serve*—*serving* you is a full-time job, oh magnificent one." He stood, bowing to her.

"Stop that!" Aminah jumped to her feet, feeling irritable. "And stop worrying about my money. I don't doubt that if I do run out, you and my last dinar will leave at the same time." She regretted her words immediately. Pain flickered in his eyes.

"If that time comes," Idris said, "I'll go back to horses and earn enough to repay your kindness."

An awkward silence stretched between them. Finally, Aminah spoke, her voice subdued. "I have sources to replenish the ducats."

Idris looked at her sharply, as though about to probe further, but then just nodded. They both settled back into silence and returned to their meal. Aminah was unhappy with herself for the hurtful things she'd said to him, and she wondered fleetingly if she ought to tell him about Jinni. *No,* she thought, *there's too much at stake.*

From their vantage point on the roof terrace, Aminah could see the garden, which was beginning to take shape under Idris's hand. She knew the key to keeping him here was to keep him busy, and Aminah was deciding on his next project when he began to speak. The strange sound of his voice brought her eyes to his face.

"Many years ago there lived in the city of Baghdad a man named Sindbad, who was so poor that he bore burdens on his head to buy his daily bread," he said, in the lilting tones of a storyteller. "One day, when the heat was oppressive and he was exceedingly weary, Sindbad stumbled under the weight of his heavy load. At that moment, he was passing the gate of a wealthy merchant's house, before which the ground was swept and watered, and there the air was temperate. He sighted a broad bench beside the door and, with a grateful sigh, Sindbad dropped his burden and sat himself down to rest and smell the cool air."

Idris paused. "That's how the story of Sindbad's first voyage begins," he said.

Stunned, Aminah hadn't taken her eyes from his face. "I . . . I know how it begins," she said. "Please, go on."

)

"YOU PROMISED we'd buy horses," said Idris.

"Oh, the price of a good story," Aminah replied. "But not today. We have to put this house in order."

"But—"

"No arguing."

Idris fell to the ground in front of her. "Don't strike me, Miss! Have mercy on your poor, humble servant."

"Oh, shut up," said Aminah, smiling. "And get to work."

With just two of them, it took the rest of the day to arrange the new furniture, lay out the carpets, and hang the tapestries. The last task was organizing the kitchen, which led to their first attempt at cooking.

They settled on the fish, fried in vinegar and sesame oil. The fish merchant had given them the recipe. Pots and utensils banged and rattled, and ingredients seemed to fly about. The room soon filled with smoke, followed by a host of unpleasant odors. When they finally plopped the unsavory mess on platters, neither of them was willing to taste it.

"It's your house," said Idris. "It's only fair that you go first."

"You're my guest," Aminah answered. "No decent host would eat before her guests."

At last they agreed to take a bite, each at the same time. Aminah was the first to spit it out in disgust.

"It's like eating carrion!" she cried, reaching for her glass of sherbet. She drank deeply to rid her mouth of the foul taste.

"How could we have turned good fish into this?" asked Idris. He wiped his tongue with a cloth. "We can try again tomorrow."

Aminah shook her head. "I'm hiring a cook."

"Wise," said Idris. "Dates and cheese?"

"I'll get them," she said. "Let's eat outside—on the terrace. The smell in here is making me sick. By the way, that's your next job."

"Getting rid of the smell?"

"No, finding a cook."

"Finding a cook? A man knows nothing of such things. That should be your job."

Aminah turned a sour eye on him.

"I'll start looking first thing tomorrow," said Idris.

)

"WAIT HERE," Aminah told the woman. She latched on to Idris's arm and dragged him across the courtyard.

"Are you out of your mind?" she whispered, when they were out of earshot.

Idris shook off her hand. "I'm doing my best. I think she's a perfect choice."

"Look at her, Idris."

They both turned to stare at the scantily dressed woman. She reminded Aminah of Rina—older, of course, but clearly plying the same trade.

"Quite pretty, don't you think?" Idris smiled and waved to her.

"Look how she's dressed—or not dressed," said Aminah. "And look at the rouge on her cheeks—she's grown past the age for that. And all those anklets, tinkling with every step."

"So?"

"Where did you find her?"

"Near a caravansary. She asked if I needed her. I asked her if she could cook. She told me she could do that, too."

Aminah laughed. "Some man of the world you are. Can't you tell a harlot from a cook?"

"She was very friendly . . ." he said, blushing.

She pressed a ducat into his hand. "Give her this. It's not that I hate harlots, but rather that I'd like someone with more practice using an oven."

After the woman was gone, Aminah took Idris in tow and headed for the main suq. She posted notices and checked the places in and about the marketplace where people needing work gathered. But no one seemed right. After two days of searching, she felt like giving up.

Then Barra arrived at the gate.

Though the woman's head was wrapped in a shawl, Aminah could tell she was at least as old as her mother. But unlike the dull, lifeless eyes she remembered from her mother's last days, Barra's were bright and full of life, and she was quick to smile.

"Young Miss," she greeted Aminah, bowing her head. "I know you are new in this house. Might your mother need someone to cook for her?" It was obvious the woman was surprised that a girl had met her at the gate.

"Did you follow me from the suq?" Aminah asked, suddenly suspicious, but the blank look in Barra's clear gaze was the only answer she needed.

Barra shook her head, and Aminah, feeling a little ashamed, returned the woman's warm smile. "I'm sorry," she said. "Please come inside."

Aminah led her into the kitchen, where they found Idris pouring himself a glass of sherbet. "This is my manservant, Idris," she said. "We are the only two in this household."

Barra raised her eyebrows.

"It is a long and sad story," Aminah said. "But I am trying to carry on with my life."

"I'm sorry, Miss. I meant no disrespect." Then Barra rounded on Idris. "What if I had been a thief? Or murderer? How could you allow your mistress to open the gate by herself? Shameful!"

For the second time since the search for a cook had begun, Idris was red-faced, and Aminah laughed. "Barra, the position is yours," she said.

The woman had nothing but what she carried in a bag slung over her shoulder, and so she moved into one of the spare suites that afternoon. Supper that night was fit for a sultan.

· Seven ·

WITH BARRA'S PRESENCE, the house seemed like a home for the first time. Though she knew the older woman couldn't protect her, Aminah somehow felt safer. And because Barra, in spite of her initial scolding, appeared to like Idris, Aminah felt more generous toward him.

At the end of Barra's first week, Aminah called Idris from the gardens and handed him a heavy leather pouch. He shook it, an ear tuned to the musical clinking of coins. "What's this for?" he asked.

"Horses," she answered, and Idris smiled.

"It's about time you paid your debt," he said.

"Now I'll see if you live up to your boasting—or if your skill with horses is but another of your stories," said Aminah, smiling in return.

"I'm sure you will not be disappointed," said Barra, coming up behind them.

"Unless she hopes I fail," said Idris.

Barra laughed. "Now why would she hope such a thing? You may accompany us to the suq, Master Idris, then it's off to the horse market with you."

Idris left them in front of Aminah's favorite hammam. She couldn't help feeling pleased with herself as she watched the spring in his gait as he hurried away. And better yet, she was about to make Barra's day one to remember.

At first Barra protested as Aminah hustled her into the

· 66 ·

hammam—not because she was against bathing, but because this was the most exclusive bathhouse in Al-Kal'as and she was ill at ease with the splendor.

"If it makes you happy," Barra finally agreed, allowing Aminah to steer her inside. But after bathing, she refused to allow the matrons of the hammam to improve her appearance with cosmetics or other adornments.

Aminah, however, decided it was time to enjoy herself. She had the matrons pluck her eyebrows and braid her hair in twenty-five plaits—weaving in silken strings from which dangled small golden disks. They brushed her with powders and anointed her with oils and perfumes. She gazed in a mirror, surprised at her emerging beauty, and wondered, *Will Idris be surprised, too?* She hoped he'd notice, at least.

Barra waited patiently until the matrons finished with Aminah, then she and her mistress descended upon the merchants of the suq. Aminah gave only a fleeting thought to attracting the guards' attention with her spending and passed the rest of a satisfying morning picking through shiny, bejeweled baubles in the gold bazaar—earrings, bracelets, and more decorations for her hair. Barra issued another polite but firm refusal when Aminah begged her to accept some for herself.

Next, they sampled every sweetmeat that caught their fancy (even Barra couldn't resist). They also stopped to watch glassblowers work their craft, and Aminah commissioned an indigo vase with a pale-blue full moon in relief. The craftsman tried to convince Aminah to choose a more popular pattern, and Barra was puzzled at her sharp insistence. "I have a strange passion for full moons," she later explained.

After that, Aminah dragged Barra into several perfumeries.

They sampled dozens of fragrances—rose, jasmine, violet, orange, lemon, and other scents captured in glistening liquid. Aminah bought them all. In the late afternoon, they combed through bookshops, picking up ancient tomes inked on parchment and newer books written on paper, filled with stories and poems, maps, and descriptions of distant places. And though Barra continued to protest, Aminah insisted she accept several new robes, sarwals, shawls, and pairs of sandals.

As the day drew to an end, Aminah stopped at a fruit stall and bought a pomegranate for each of them. The vendors had promised to deliver their packages that evening, so they strolled unburdened to the suq's fountain, where a snake charmer was hard at work. His swaying cobra, its hood fanned, made Barra's skin crawl, and she hurriedly pulled Aminah past.

"We should go home," said Barra, glancing back at the snake. "It's time to cook our evening meal."

But Aminah wasn't quite ready to leave. Her attention was on a storyteller, weaving the tale of Ali Baba. Aminah coaxed ruby seeds from the pomegranate while she listened, wondering how Idris might tell the same story. But she was soon distracted by the bobbing peacock feather on the man's turban and lost track of the tale.

"Not so good," Barra whispered. "Let's move along."

Aminah nodded, yet she dropped a silver dirham in the storyteller's basket as they left.

The wares of another vendor caught Aminah's eye a moment later. She ran her fingers over black and white chessmen lined up on a black-and-white inlaid board, and bittersweet memories made her reach into her money belt.

"Now, Miss, what do you need that for?" asked Barra. "Do you even play?"

"Do I play?" Aminah smiled, a distant look in her eye. "Yes, I'm quite good. My father taught me. On cool desert nights, we spent hours playing under the stars."

"Will Idris be your partner now?" asked Barra. "It won't be your faithful cook, I can tell you that much. She doesn't know the first thing about the game."

"If Idris doesn't know chess, then I'll teach him," she answered. "I imagine the cook can learn, too."

"Your cook is too old and too stubborn."

"We'll see," said Aminah.

Finally, Barra was able to steer her mistress toward home, but as they were about to exit the suq, Aminah was drawn to yet another stall. Small enclosures hung from poles and flittered with sound and color. With Barra clucking her tongue, Aminah chose a pair of red and yellow finches in a wicker cage.

"Another pair of mouths to feed," said Barra, in quiet reproof. "Rather feed the city's orphans."

A sharp retort reached Aminah's lips, but she bit it back as a vision from her street life leapt into her mind. She shuddered at the memory of a little boy—she'd never learned his name—whose tiny, lifeless husk she'd found huddled against the city wall, flies covering his face.

Aminah shook her head angrily to dispel the image. Why should she feel guilty about her change in fortune? And what was the point of having all this gold if she couldn't spend it as she pleased? Without a word, she paid for the finches and shoved the chess set into Barra's hands. She took up the birdcage and started down the street, Barra trailing silently behind.

When they arrived at Aminah's suite, Barra placed the game box on the cushions of the diwan. "Thank you, Miss," she said, without looking up, "for a nice day. And please forgive an old woman's loose tongue." Then she left for her quarters, shaking her head as she went.

As Aminah watched her go, she flushed with shame. She'd acted like a spoiled princess—the kind of behavior she hated. The streets had hardened her to the opinions of others, but for some reason it was different with Barra. It was almost as if a parent had passed judgment on her.

She shut the door and flopped down on the diwan, engulfed in gloom.

)

"I NEVER SHOULD HAVE TOLD you about the lamp," said Aladdin. "Now you'll tear Al-Kal'as apart looking for it."

"Never told me!" Badr al-Budur glared at her prince. "If you'd told me to begin with, we'd still have it."

"If *you'd* controlled your temper, we'd still have it. The lamp was special to me, I told you that much. Yet you tossed it out the window."

Badr grabbed her ivory hairbrush and flung it at Aladdin. He ducked, and it bounced off the wall behind him.

"I'll find that beggar girl," said the Princess. "She'll pay for stealing my lamp."

"You gave her the lamp," he said. "Besides, we're not certain she ended up with it. You knocked her senseless, after all. Maybe it lay in the street until someone else found it. And if the girl does have the lamp, then good for her. She ought to have a chance to let it change her life—just as it changed mine."

"And what sort of life did you lead that needed so much changing?" The Princess's face was a mask of contempt. "No, don't tell me. I might be sick."

Aladdin's eyes narrowed, but he answered in an even tone. "I hope whoever has the lamp is wiser than I was."

"What do you mean by that?" Badr shook her tiny fist in his face. "You're nothing without your jinni. Nothing! Should I tell my father the truth? That you consort with demons? That you pretend to be something you aren't?"

Aladdin shrugged. "I am what I am now. I have riches. I have influence. I am a prince. Besides, would your father believe such a tale?"

"He'd listen to his own daughter."

"But he likes me better than his own daughter, my dear."

The Prince dodged another brush.

"Oh, yes, he likes you," said Badr. "That's why he's sending you to Baghdad for a year. To get rid of you."

"The Sultan trusts me. I'm his emissary."

The Princess laughed, but her bitter outburst faded as a voice called through the curtained doorway. Recognizing the Captain of the Guard, she stepped forward to part the drapery.

"What are you doing here?" she asked, covering her face with a silk hijab.

"Pardon me, Princess, but I must see you and Prince Aladdin," Saladin answered, bowing. "The servant girl Fatimah let me in. Forgive the intrusion, but I am here on two missions."

"Get on with it, then," said Aladdin.

Saladin bowed again. "First, the Sultan wishes me to escort his only child into his most exalted presence. Second, you are late for your meeting with the caravan chief, Prince Aladdin."

Aladdin slapped his forehead, and without so much as another glance at Badr, he hurried from the apartment.

"What does my father want?" asked Badr, a frown wrinkling her forehead. "Whenever he summons me, it's usually unpleasant."

"I know not, Princess."

"Why did Father send you on such a petty errand?" Badr asked. "Don't you have more pressing business?"

"I volunteered, Princess."

"I'm suspicious of volunteers, Saladin," she said. "I need a moment to change. Wait by the outer door."

When the Captain of the Guard didn't move, Badr stopped loosening her sash, turning an indignant eye on him. "Do you plan to watch me undress?"

She expected him to blush, to back out of the room in embarrassed haste, but his steely eyes didn't even blink. His chiseled features inscrutable, he stood in silence—tall, broad-shouldered, immovable—and Badr felt a brief tingle of fear.

Saladin cleared his throat. "May I speak, Princess?" he asked.

"If you must," she answered.

The Captain stepped closer, lowering his voice. "Aladdin is a fine fellow."

Badr suppressed the urge to move back. "What do you want?"

"Your father is aging. His health is poor. Though Aladdin is a fine fellow, the Sultan's own blood ought to succeed him."

Badr's head came up. "I never thought it fair I was born a girl," she said, unable to keep the bitterness from her voice. "I'm smarter and more iron-willed than the bumbling men in Father's court."

"This I have observed," said Saladin. "You would make a better ruler than your father—and your husband. I would be pleased to serve you."

Now the Princess stepped closer. "What do you want?" she asked again.

"It is what you want that is my concern," he said. "I can help you find the lamp."

"You were listening to us! I ought to have your ears cut off for eavesdropping."

"Once you have the lamp, it will not matter that you are a daughter and not a son. With the jinni's power, you can revise tradition. The people will accept you without question."

"What do you want?" Badr asked for the third time.

"I would be your Grand Vizier," he answered. "And if something were to happen to Aladdin, then perhaps . . . even more."

Badr was surprised at his boldness, but even more surprised that the idea didn't seem repulsive to her. "You will be my Grand Vizier," she said, lowering her hijab. "As for anything beyond that, only time will tell. How do I know you won't keep the lamp for yourself?"

"I am bound by the hope, slight as it may be, that you will be mine," he answered.

The Full Moon of Full Moons smiled, and Saladin's heart quickened.

Second Moon

· Eight ·

AMINAH SAT ON HER DIWAN and stared out the window. Barra was already in her quarters, and Idris was out on an evening ride, so she sat alone. The sky promised Aminah's second full moon since finding the lamp. In just a little while, she could summon Jinni again.

She gazed across her small estate, adding her sigh to the soft sounds of a breeze rustling in the palms and sandalwoods. By most accounts, she should have been happy. Since the last moon she had acquired a home; she would never have to sleep on the streets again. She didn't have to worry about her clothes wearing out or where her next meal would come from. She had two companions to help her ward off loneliness and danger. She had managed to elude Badr's clutches so far. And with Jinni's help, she could increase her wealth, comfort, and security.

But one thing continued to plague her. Aminah was still beset by unsettling dreams. She was haunted by images of children who had lived with her in the streets—little Abdulla and his ragged sister, Darirah, their faces and arms covered with weeping sores. In the nightmares, she also saw men without arms or legs begging at street corners or abandoned women rooting through garbage for food. She even dreamed of finding Rina in an alley, her throat slit and a knife buried in her breast.

Aminah had tried to shake off these visions by staying busy

around the house, helping Idris with the horses, and shopping for food with Barra. But one day she discovered that going to the marketplace only made things worse, because there her dreams and reality converged.

As they were leaving the suq, Barra suddenly left Aminah's side to lift a small, crumpled heap from the alley filth. The heap was a little girl, and Aminah immediately noticed her bloated stomach—the illusion of a full belly shared by starving children—and her hollow eyes. Her mother squatted in the dust nearby, too weak in the blistering heat to go to her daughter.

On impulse, Aminah turned to run, as if to escape the memory of her own bloated stomach. She'd taken only a few steps when she came to her senses and stopped.

From a distance, Aminah watched Barra feed the girl and her mother with bread she'd been carrying home from the marketplace. Then Barra secretly tucked not one but all of her hard-earned silver dirhams into the woman's limp hand.

Except for Hassan, no one had ever done something like this for Aminah, and so the sight of Barra's unselfishness and compassion rent her heart. When the starving woman began to weep in gratitude, Aminah stumbled forward, sobbing and unloading her money belt.

But the jingling of coins was a call to action for every beggar within range of the sound. As if they'd dropped from the sky, sallow-faced men and women surrounded Aminah in an instant. They cried out, clutching at her and plucking dinars from her fingers. The faster she rid herself of the coins, the more she realized how little help they were—there were just too many people. Aminah recalled Jinni's words, "We jinn cannot fix the world," and grimaced—she couldn't even fix the trouble on this street.

Her money belt was soon empty, but the throng didn't seem to notice. They tugged at her garments, begging for more, until she was in danger of being dragged to the ground. Barra reached into the mob to grasp the neck of Aminah's thawb and pulled her backward into an empty alley.

"Run!" Barra cried, and they both bolted for home.

In the safety of her quarters, Aminah thought about that afternoon's scare. She couldn't blame the beggars. As Barra pointed out, Aminah was responsible for the frenzy herself. That much gold thrown open to desperate people—well, it was to be expected.

To erase the memory of the little girl's distended belly, Aminah surrounded herself with the books, maps, and manuscripts she'd purchased in the suq. The smells of paper and ink turned her thoughts to her father. She remembered him bringing home maps. He'd spread them out on the floor and take her on tours of distant, exotic places. The light in his eyes as he described Makkah, Tyre, Baghdad, or the great Mediterranean Sea was what she remembered most. Her father had spent his days reading about the world for the Sultan, and yet he had never been able to see much of it.

"Someday, little one," he'd say, "we'll wade in the sea. I promise." She had held that dream in her heart—until starvation and death had withered away hope.

Suddenly, Aminah realized she could fulfill her childhood dreams—with the help of her jinni. If she couldn't change Al-Kal'as, then she could escape it! Temporarily, at least.

Aminah turned back to the window, willing the wishing moon to rise. She fidgeted with unbridled excitement until the great golden orb rolled lazily above the trees, then she ran to fetch the lamp from its hiding place. With a shaking hand, she touched the small star engraved on its spout, moving her fingers to feel the matching mark on her forehead. She took a deep breath, rubbed the brass surface with brisk circular motions, and set the lamp on the floor.

It sputtered and belched purple smoke. It hopped and clattered about the room, bumping into walls and battering Aminah's shins. When at last the lamp came to rest, Jinni exploded from the spout in a wild display of fireworks, but what should have been a bone-rattling bang was no more than a small pop. The demon's great body swelled until it almost filled the room.

"Ask whatso thou wantest, for I am the Slave—" He paused, his face wrinked in disgust. "For I am the Slave of whoso hath the lamp."

Aminah was relieved to hear the much-reduced level of his voice. "Don't you remember?" she asked. "I told you to stop saying *whatso* and *whoso*. Keep it simple—no flowery language required. And you don't need to call yourself a slave. It's obvious you don't like it."

"And I told you that you would have to wish it." Jinni crossed his arms and struck a stubborn pose.

Aminah shrugged. "Have it your way. Even though you insist on being rude, I still want to thank you for the ducats—but you might have warned me that I'd have trouble spending them. And carrying them."

Jinni snickered. His laughter had a nasty edge to it. "You

did not specify what sort of gold coins, and so—" Suddenly his face lightened, and he shrank to human size. "You thanked me."

"Of course," she said. "Look around. You've done wonders for a starving beggar girl. It wouldn't be right not to thank you. Two thousand thank yous, in fact."

Aminah thought she saw a smile flutter across the demon's lips, though she couldn't be certain. "Noble jinni of the lamp, may I use my wishes?" she asked.

Jinni's head came up at the word noble, and this time the brief smile was unmistakable. He folded into a deep bow and said, "Ask whatso thou wantest."

Aminah paused, making certain she chose the right words. "I want to travel to any time and place in the blink of an eye. I want to imagine a place and a time, wish myself there, and poof! There I'll be! Past, present, future. Can you do that?"

"Can I do that? Of course, I can do that! Do you think me a neophyte, a bumbler, a charlatan?"

"I'm new at this," said Aminah. "I didn't know."

"Humans," Jinni grumbled. He ballooned to twice his size, sucking in a vast amount of air as he grew. "To hear is to obey!" he tried to shout. But the words were only as loud as if he were having a casual conversation.

A disappointed frown settled over his face and his body deflated. He clenched his teeth and swelled to three times his size, filling his demon lungs to the point that his chest seemed ready to burst.

"To hear is to obey!" he screamed. "To hear is to obey!" But the shrieking that came from his mouth was no more than a whisper.

Jinni shrank again, diminishing until he was Aminah's size. "Thy wish is granted," he said in a dull voice. "Close thine eyes and imagine where and when, and thou shalt be there."

Aminah felt a tickle behind her breastbone. "Thank you," she said.

"A thousand curses!" Jinni cried. He stomped and kicked about the room, but the volume of his oaths couldn't match his anger. "The louder I yell, the quieter it comes out! How can I exist without shouting and roaring? It is a hallmark of the jinn and one of our very few pleasures, and you have taken it from me with your mindless wish for quiet."

"You're blaming me?" Aminah shook her head in disbelief. "You did it to yourself, demon. Serves you right for tricking me into wasting a wish. As the old saying goes, he who digs a hole for his brother will fall into it. Looks like you fell in face first."

Smoke streamed from Jinni's ears, and a rich reddish-purple rose into his cheeks.

"Don't take it so hard," said Aminah. "It could have happened to anyone."

"Yes," said Jinni, brightening. "It happened to you, Miss. Two wasted wishes in a row, as I recall. Colossal stupidity!"

Indignant, Aminah opened her mouth to protest but ended up laughing instead. "You win, Jinni," she said.

"Of course I won," he said. "I always do."

"Yes, well, thank you for granting my wish."

Jinni scowled. "Be warned, Miss. If you relinquish possession of the lamp, wishes of this sort terminate. Gold you may keep or other material things—even enchanted devices—but not magical powers. Lose the lamp, and you are stranded in Baghdad, Rome, or New York City."

"New York City?"

"Never mind," said Jinni. "I forgot that you know nothing of the future." He tugged on his earring, looking at Aminah with troubled eyes. "What is the matter with me? I never give warnings about wishes."

"You must like me."

"Rubbish! Jinn care for no one."

"No, I think you like me, Jinni. Go on, admit it."

"Like you? Care about a smelly, scrawny girl who crawled from the sewers? I think not."

Aminah laughed again. "Open your eyes, Jinni. I've bathed since we last met. And added some flesh, thanks to you." She pirouetted, showing off her budding figure.

Jinni sniffed. "Nevertheless . . ."

"Thank you, anyway," she said. "I'll be sure to remember your advice."

"Humans are too stupid to heed my advice, so I suppose I should not worry about giving it."

"You can't be nice, can you?"

Jinni didn't answer. His eyes were locked on her new chessboard that was displayed on a low table across the room.

"Do you play chess?" asked Aminah.

"If thou *wishest* to know the answer—"

"Cranky bottle imp!" Aminah cried. "I'm not wasting a wish, though you'd love that. It was only a friendly question."

Jinni turned various shades of purple. "Insults! I will tolerate no more." He began to dissolve, flowing into the spout, but suddenly he stopped, the lower half of his body inside the lamp. "I am certain I was a master of the game," he said, stroking his beard, deep in thought, "though it is difficult to remember. I have not touched a board in aeons."

"My father loved the game," said Aminah.

"It seems to me that I loved it, too."

The puzzled look on the demon's face reminded Aminah of her father puzzling over a chess move. But this look was also unhappy, and she felt a moment of pity for him.

"Ivory chessmen," Jinni said to himself. "Excellent quality. Yes, I think I remember owning such a set. If so, where is it?"

"You may go now," said Aminah, anxious to try her new powers. "I'll see you again soon."

Still lost in thought, Jinni dissolved into a fine mist—tinged the color of ripe plums—and seeped into the lamp without another word.

She watched the last of the vapors drift away, and then, taking account of Jinni's warning, she strung the lamp onto a strong leather cord and threaded it beneath her robe. With the cord secured at her waist, Aminah stepped to the center of the room and closed her eyes.

"Where should I go?" she wondered aloud. Not only where but also when?

Sudden images of time travel weakened her knees, and her eyes snapped open. What if she bumped into herself in the future? Or discovered something awful was going to happen to Idris or Barra? Or to herself, for that matter? It had sounded grand when she'd made her wish, but now that she was facing the reality, passing through time was terrifying. She stumbled over to the diwan and collapsed on its cushions.

Start with something simple, Aminah told herself. She stood again and took a deep breath. Closing her eyes once more, she pictured the rock outcropping where she'd hidden the ducats. Imagining herself looking down on a sandstone ledge she remembered, Aminah wished herself there.

The air about her grew cold. Her skin prickled, and the hair on her arms and neck stood on end. With a dizzying jerk, she was pulled from the room. In the blink of an eye, she fell out of the air, crashing against the stone surface and tumbling down the slope. She landed a few paces away from where she had buried her treasure.

Spitting sand, Aminah groaned and struggled to her feet. She wiggled her fingers, moved her arms and legs, and rotated her ankles. Except for bruises and scrapes, she wasn't hurt, though her sarwal had a hole in one knee and the sharp rocks had shredded the back of her robe.

She managed a rueful laugh. "Next time, imagine yourself *sitting* on the rock, Aminah. Not floating above it." Then she closed her eyes, shutting out the cool light of the full moon, and pictured herself back in her quarters—standing with both feet on the floor. After another icy, electric jolt, Aminah was relieved to see she was back where she'd begun.

After she'd cleaned her scrapes and changed her clothes, Aminah felt a little braver and decided it was time to wade in the sea. To touch and taste and smell its salty waves. But then she realized that she'd never seen the sea. How could she imagine what she'd never seen? It would take more than thinking of salt water to be transported there. She needed to know a particular sea, and she didn't.

Aminah stamped her foot in anger. The jinni had tricked

her again. She could only picture in her mind what she'd experienced, and her experiences were limited to Al-Kal'as. All she could do was travel back and forth across town, no farther into time than back through her own fourteen years.

She grabbed the lamp and gave it a horrible shaking, which produced a few tiny puffs of lavender smoke. Then she threw herself on the diwan, shoving the books and papers to the floor, and covered her face with a pillow. She wanted to scream, but as she opened her mouth, an idea flashed through her head like a brilliant streak of light.

Aminah snatched up one of the books and started leafing through the pages. In a tome on world geography, she read a vivid description of the port city of Tyre and studied its location on a chart of the Mediterranean Sea. Then, remembering the words, she painted a picture of Tyre in her mind's eye and thought of its spot on the map.

Satisfied, she double-checked the lamp and the ducats in her money belt, then shut her eyes. Bringing back the image of Tyre, she wished to be there. In a dizzying moment, she was.

Aminah opened her eyes to find herself standing on the quay, looking out on the moon-streaked sea, just as a drawing in the book had shown. The sleeping city lay behind her, but she could not pull her eyes from the water. She breathed in the salty air and walked along the quay, looking for a place where she could touch the waves.

Deciding she wanted privacy, Aminah left the harbor and followed the streets until she found a city gate. Leaving Tyre, she walked along the shore, traveling far enough away from town to feel alone. Then she removed her cloak, drew up the legs of her sarwal, and removed her sandals.

As she crossed the beach and neared the dark water, Aminah shivered with anticipation. The sand grew cool and damp, hard and rippled, and then a wave broke over her naked feet. She squealed in delight. It was magical, as magical as anything the jinn could conjure, and she felt sudden and unexpected gratitude to Allah for creating such enchantments.

Aminah waded up to her knees, dipped a hand in the water, and brought her fingers to her lips. The bitter taste was a surprise, even though she thought she knew what to expect.

As she stood with waves lapping at her thighs, she knew she wanted more from the sea than wet legs. She hurried out of the water, stripped away her trousers, shirt, and undergarments, and returned to bathe in the briny surf. The salt stung her eyes, burned her scraped flesh, and made her feel alive. Bathing in the open should have been unthinkable, especially naked, but Aminah didn't care. She was caught in the sea's spell.

Hours later, she dried herself in the breeze and dressed, then sat on a knoll above the beach to watch the sun rise. Soon seagulls wheeled in the cerulean sky, landing to squawk and squabble over tasty morsels. She walked along the sand, picking up shells and driftwood or kneeling to examine strange little creatures scuttling in the surf.

Entranced, Aminah lost track of time, but as she drew near Tyre, the meuzzin's call for afternoon prayer was a shocking reminder. By now Barra, even Idris, would have mounted a frantic search for her.

Aminah rearranged her clothing and slipped on her sandals, wondering if she had to go back to the exact spot where she'd arrived in order to return home. That would delay her even more. She decided to stay where she was and stood still, imagining herself back in her suite in Al-Kal'as. The same hair-raising jolt threw her from the beach, and she landed, scattering sand, in the middle of her room.

"Barra," she called, running for the door. "Idris, I'm here." Her voice trailed away. Outside her window, the sky was black.

She left her quarters and skirted the moonlit courtyard, soon arriving at the stable. One of the stallions was still gone.

"It's as if I'd never been away," she murmured.

· Nine ·

THAT NIGHT, rather than children's emaciated faces, Aminah dreamed of ocean swells and screeching seagulls, and she awoke refreshed and determined to visit someplace new.

After breakfast, she pulled Idris aside. "You've been to the sea, I suppose?" she asked.

"No," he answered. "I'm not from here, but that doesn't mean I'm a world traveler. I've always imagined riding horses down a sandy beach, though. Or at least, what I imagine a sandy beach to be." Idris paused, his eyes narrowing. "Why are you asking about the sea? Are you leaving Al-Kal'as?"

"Worried I'll go without you?" she asked. "If you awake and find me gone, now you'll have some idea where to look."

"And I *will* find you—to drown you in salt water, if for no other reason. Just try leaving me behind."

"Why, Idris, you'd miss me that much—to kill me in a fit of desperate loneliness?" Aminah laughed.

"I'd miss your ducats, at least," he said. "Look, why don't we take some of those ducats and join a caravan going west? We'll taste the sea—and afterward, visit other places. What do you say?"

"Someday, perhaps," she answered. "If those horses don't eat me into the almshouse first. I think I'll start by reading about the sea. And about the holy cities. Come with me to Zayn, the bookseller, and I'll see what I can find."

"You only want me along so you'll have a packhorse to carry

your books, if he has any left to sell. You cleared Zayn's tables last week. Nevertheless, he'll smile to see you coming."

"Just like the feed-and-saddle vendor smiles when he sees you coming," said Aminah, giving him a playful shove.

It took them only an hour to fill a cart with books and maps and start for home, Idris dragging the load behind him. Aminah trailed the cart, leafing through a volume about the holy city of Makkah.

"Why the sudden interest in Makkah?" Idris asked, stopping to look at her. "Are you thinking of becoming religious?"

"Are you saying I'm a nonbeliever?"

"Sure. One look at you and anyone can tell you're a real heathen. A colossal doubter."

Aminah smiled and made to throw the book at him. "I'd split your skull with this, but I don't want to get blood on it."

Disarmed by his wide smile, Aminah suddenly found herself confiding in him. "I've been having terrible nightmares," she said.

Idris's smile disappeared.

"The faces of dead children. Starving babies and their mothers. Horrible things, and I don't know how to stop them." Aminah paused, remembering the rush of feelings for Allah on Tyre's beaches and the pleasant dreams that had followed. "I thought finding out more about God and the holy cities might help somehow."

"Have you considered the hajj?" asked Idris, soberly. "As a way to cleanse your mind? I hear the pilgrimage to Makkah can change one's life."

The idea of the sacred hajj had been at the back of Aminah's mind since returning from Tyre. Her father had always talked of making the pilgrimage, but until now she had never given it much thought. She was surprised that Idris would suggest it—he didn't seem the religious type himself—and for a moment she considered asking him to make the trip with her. But then she'd have to reveal the lamp, and Aminah was not ready for that.

"No," she answered, refusing to feel guilty for the lie. "No, it's much too far, and the travel much too dangerous."

Idris yanked on the cart handle and started forward again. "Reading won't help rid you of nightmares. You must take action!" he said, punching at the air. "Let's go to Makkah!"

"Perhaps someday," said Aminah. "When I'm braver."

Idris dropped his shoulders in disappointment and trudged on in silence. When they arrived at her quarters, he dumped the load in the middle of her floor and hurried off to the stables. As he left, he threw her an odd look, as if to say how pitiful she was to be so timid. *If only he knew how adventurous I really am,* she thought.

But Aminah almost changed her mind about going when she discovered that the hajj could be performed only during the Month of the Pilgrimage, which had long since passed. That meant she would have to try her hand at time travel, and though going back a few months didn't seem much of a risk, she was apprehensive.

During the next several days, as she read everything she could find on Makkah and the hajj, Aminah's anxiety was replaced by anticipation. Certain now that she'd make the trip, she went to the suq to purchase an ihram, the seamless white robe worn by all pilgrims. Then, after making certain the lamp was locked up tight, she packed a small satchel with a few necessities—a little food, some extra clothing—and waited until everyone in the house was asleep.

Aminah stood in the middle of the room and opened one of her books to a map of Arabia that showed the location of Makkah. She closed her eyes and envisioned the pilgrims gathered at the border of the sanctuary, ready to begin the hajj. She held in her thoughts the seventh day of the Month of the Pilgrimage, a day gone by five months ago. As the air grew cold, she tossed the book aside.

As usual, her skin prickled and her hair stood on end, but then the spinning sensation that always made her dizzy picked up speed. Faster and faster her mind spun, as if her brain had been drawn into a whirlwind. As she was about to lose consciousness, Aminah found herself on her knees, throwing up Barra's supper.

Jinni's revenge! The dazed thought slid through her mind between retches, and she was certain he'd known what time travel would do to her.

As Aminah finally managed to turn her head and squint through blurry eyes, she noticed the flickering yellow light of a fire that danced on the surface of a pilgrim's nearby tent. Hidden from view by the darkness, she stood to get a better look at her surroundings. She was at the edge of a veritable city of tents that stretched across the plains. Firelight dotted the landscape, and she could hear the pilgrims calling to one another, excitement tingeing their voices. Men and women, some already dressed in ihrams, were suddenly illuminated as they crossed in front of their cooking pits.

As Aminah stared in awe, an unintelligible shout from nearby startled her. She dropped back to the ground, certain someone must have spotted her. The deep voice cried out again, and this time the words were clear. "Nazreen, light a lamp!"

Aminah jumped up to run, but she was still too woozy. Instead, she crouched behind a thornbush. From her hiding place, she could hear the repeated striking of flint and a mild exclamation. The heavy fabric of the tent took on a faint luminescent quality just before someone flew from the opening and lay sprawled before the fire. Her tense muscles relaxed. They weren't after her.

A giant of a man marched from the tent and knelt over the prostrate figure, keeping it pinned to the ground with one massive hand. A woman came next, carrying a lamp. *Nazreen,* Aminah thought.

The giant grasped the figure—a young man—by the arm, hoisting him to his feet with no more effort than lifting a kitten. "What are you called, boy?"

Aminah was disarmed by the gentleness in the giant's voice. The boy answered without hesitating. "Hasim," he said. "And I'm no boy."

"No? Then I suppose you think being a thief makes you a man?"

"Shall I get help, Talib?" Nazreen asked.

"No, wife. There's no need."

Aminah wondered at his calmness. Curiosity piqued, she moved to a closer bush and could see that Hasim was, indeed, on the cusp of manhood. He stood nearly as tall as the older man but carried less than half the bulk.

"Well, Hasim, what were you doing in our tent?" Talib asked.

"I . . . I wasn't stealing," Hasim stammered. "I was hoping to trade this for something to eat. And for a few dinars." He pointed to a rolled-up bundle that lay beside the tent.

As Nazreen kept a wary eye on Hasim, Talib untied the bundle and unrolled it.

"By Allah," Talib said, whistling softly. "I know carpets, and this is as fine as I've seen." His fingers stroked its tight weave. "Where did you get it?"

"I didn't steal it, if that's what you're thinking," Hasim said. "I made the rug myself."

Talib raised his eyebrows.

"You wove this yourself?" asked Nazreen, who had joined her husband. "Then why not sell it, if you are in need?"

Aminah stretched her neck to get a better look at the rug.

"Don't you think I tried?" asked Hasim. He seemed close to tears. "Everyone in Makkah thinks I stole it, too. Some even tried turning me over to the city guards, so I ran into the wilderness."

"Have you no family in the holy city?" asked Nazreen. Aminah sensed a note of sympathy in her voice.

Hasim shook his head. "Since I can remember, I have lived and worked with Master," he said. "He taught me to weave but said I wasn't much good at it—and never would be. But I knew better. By the time I was twelve, my rugs always sold first. I think it made him angry."

"So you've run away from your master," said Talib. "Little wonder you fear the guards. The punishment will be harsh."

Man and boy stood in silence for a few seconds, pondering Hasim's future. Finally, Talib spoke. "I will purchase your carpet. I will give you two thousand dinars."

Aminah gasped, then clasped a hand over her mouth. Nazreen only smiled and nodded.

"But it is so small a rug," said Hasim.

"One thousand now, the other thousand upon meeting one condition—return home to Aleppo with us and begin afresh."

"How could I? We have only just met—"

"Because it is better than whatever else lies ahead of you. Your skill is plain to see, Hasim. Now you will have money for a loom. I will help find you a small space to rent. In no time you will be a success."

"And then what will you want of me?" asked Hasim, his body rigid with distrust. "Half of all I earn, or more? What is your game?" He backed away.

Talib reached out and grabbed Hasim's wrist before he could flee, then pulled a pouch from beneath his robe as the boy struggled to escape. "Hasim, life can become knotted, tangled, and thus seem hopeless. But for every knot there is someone to undo it. Nazreen and I would be honored to begin the undoing of yours. I have read your heart, my young weaver, and know we will have invested well. He who chews with his own teeth benefits himself, as the old proverb goes, and you will be chewing very soon. But because of what you are, you will not only benefit yourself, Hasim. You will also benefit others."

Hasim looked as puzzled as Aminah felt. What did this gentle giant mean? Was this just a business deal, or was Talib truly offering something more?

"Starting a new venture is always difficult," Talib continued, his soft voice causing Hasim's body to relax. "But a journey of a thousand leagues begins with one step. So do not fear the future, my boy. There! One thousand dinars. The rest is yours when we set up your new business."

As the pouch dropped into his palm, Aminah saw a flicker in Hasim's eyes. She hoped it was joy and gratitude, not greed.

"First Nazreen and I are going to complete the hajj. You must join us," Talib insisted. When he saw the doubt on Hasim's face, he added. "Do not fear the guards. You will accompany us as a son. In the morning, you will take the first step of your journey."

"Thank you," said Hasim, tears beginning to mark his cheeks. "Thank you." He threw his arms around Talib, then Nazreen, who beamed with pleasure.

Aminah found herself dabbing her own eyes. The couple's kindness wrapped about her like a warm blanket on a cold night.

When the new day dawned—the first day of the hajj— Aminah followed Talib, Nazreen, and Hasim into the miles of sanctuary that surrounded Makkah, moving forward to the village of Mina. She slept under the stars again that night, near Talib's tent so she could watch them.

On the second day, the throng of pilgrims flowed onto the Plain of Arafat where, she had learned, one might get closest to Allah. Some stood there for hours, facing Makkah, meditating and praying. Aminah joined them, though she and many others chose to sit. "Doubly at Thy service, oh God," she repeated, along with the rest.

But try as she might, Aminah found she couldn't concentrate on the events of the hajj. Something profound had happened the night before, as Talib had dealt with Hasim, and she was struggling to piece it together for herself. Aminah felt she wouldn't understand until she knew how Hasim's story ended. Only then would the pieces of the puzzle fall into place.

Later in the day, a great number of pilgrims rose from the dust of the plain and began to climb the Mount of Mercy, the sacred spot from which the Prophet Muhammad had spoken his Farewell Sermon. Though Talib, along with his wife and new son, joined the ascent, Aminah held back. For her, the hajj was over.

She wandered a safe distance away, out of sight in a gully. She braced herself for the rough ride forward through time, and then she imagined herself standing in her quarters. As she appeared in her room, the book she'd tossed aside two days before hit the floor with a bang.

Aminah threw up all over it.

· Ten ·

AMINAH FELL onto the diwan and lay there until she felt stable enough to stand. She cleaned up after herself, then crossed the room to her books and rummaged through them until she found a map and a description of Aleppo.

It would be useless to arrive in Aleppo while it was still dark, so Aminah waited until the blackness outside her window faded into gray. Then she changed out of her ihram and leapt six months into the future, arriving just before the city awakened. She vomited again, but once the sun was up, she felt well enough to begin inquiring about a carpet maker named Hasim. She expected a long day before finding him. Fortunately, the fourth merchant Aminah asked was able to direct her to his shop.

She followed the man's instructions and found a modest storefront space that was sufficiently wide and deep. A professionally lettered sign announced that this was HASIM'S FINE CARPETS.

Aminah hardly recognized Hasim. Tall and well-groomed—and smartly dressed—he looked less a boy and more a successful young merchant. But most amazing to her was the small troop of boys—even a girl or two—who worked at the looms or at other tasks. She recognized the hungry look of street orphans.

Checking to be sure her hijab was well in place, she entered the shop and began examining the carpets. Hasim left the boy he was instructing at one of the looms and hurried to her side. "I wish we had more to show you, Madam," he said, "but we've only been in business a few months."

"This one is exceptional," Aminah said. "Did your young workers weave it?"

Hasim smiled. "No," he said. "I did that myself. But the little ones are learning. They live with me above the factory. There is room enough for all of us and more. It is my way of repaying the world for my good fortune."

Aminah let the carpet slip from her fingers as the final puzzle pieces clicked into their proper places. Now she understood. *Well done, Hasim,* she said to herself. *Talib judged you rightly.*

❯

AMINAH APPEARED back in her quarters carrying a small prayer rug. Hasim had protested when she hadn't haggled with him over the price. She'd insisted on paying the amount he'd originally asked, plus a little extra. Even then, it wasn't nearly enough for the lesson he and Talib had taught her.

After stowing the rug in a corner, Aminah opened the hidden room and took out the lamp. She gave it a rub and quickly held it at arm's length, but this time the lamp sat in her hands, benign and unmoving. Jinni, looking rather cranky, billowed from the spout.

"Ask whatso thou wantest," he said, his voice sullen.

"Hello, Jinni."

He raised a purple eyebrow. "Hello? Is that all you have to say to me? Could you have shaken the lamp with more violence? I am fortunate to be in one piece, Miss!"

Aminah had forgotten about shaking the lamp—it seemed

so long ago. She shrugged apologetically. "I thought you'd tricked me again."

"But I did not trick you," he said.

"No, but you could have warned me to be careful. I almost broke my neck coming down on a rock. And when I leapt back in time, I thought my head was going to explode. And my stomach—"

"You should have asked," Jinni interrupted.

"Fine. I'm sorry for shaking the lamp. Now will you tell me about time travel?"

"As you wish."

"Oh no. You're not doing that to me again," Aminah said, bristling. "This is not a wish."

Jinni sighed. "All you need to know is that you will grow accustomed to it. The sickness will be less intense each time."

"And the farther back or forward I go, the sicker I'll get?"

Jinni shrugged.

"What's that supposed to mean?" asked Aminah. "Don't tell me you don't know. Oh, that's just marvelous! I've got a jinni who hasn't read the book of instructions."

Jinni whirled about like a top, spinning until he was a blur of color, then stopped in an instant. His teeth grew sharper, his ears more pointed, and then he shot upward, a nasty shade of purple coursing through his body, until he towered over her.

"No, wait. I'm sorry," Aminah said. "If you don't know, you don't know."

"I am not a seasoned jinni," he said, sounding grumpy, as he shrank to human size. "Some jinn have had a thousand years of practice. I have only been at it for a few hundred—or so I am told."

"You don't remember?"

Jinni shook his head.

The demon looked so forlorn that once again Aminah couldn't help feeling sorry for him. She reached out and patted his shoulder. He looked up in surprise.

Aminah slowly pulled back her hand, but he hadn't seemed to mind her touch. Uncomfortable with the silence that stretched between them, she cleared her throat and said, "I'd like to make a wish now. I still have two, right?"

Jinni nodded. "Ask whatso thou wantest," he said.

"Idris seems to worry about running out of gold, so I'd like a money box. One that stays full of dinars, no matter how much or how often I take from it."

"Will you tell him of this box?" asked Jinni.

"No, of course not. But I'll tell him that my money is endless. I'll give him all he wants."

"Ah," said Jinni. "Then the thief will have no reason to steal."

"I didn't say that. Anyway, that's my wish. And no tricks, please."

"It shall be done," said Jinni, snapping his fingers.

A square box the size of both Idris's horses landed in the corner of the room, smashing a huge clay pot. "Smaller!" she cried.

The giant cube vanished, leaving behind a well-crafted box of teakwood, banded in silver and small enough for Aminah to carry. She opened the lid and ran her fingers through the coins. She took a handful, and gold pieces boiled up from the bottom to fill the depression.

"Thank you," she said, but her purple demon didn't answer. Aminah looked up from the gold in her hands to find him staring across the room. "Jinni!"

He turned a sour face to her and said, "I suppose you have another wish."

"What's wrong now?" Aminah asked. "You seem angry."

"It matters not," Jinni answered, with a dismissive wave of his hand. "Get on with it. And if it pleases you, I would return to the lamp when the wishing is done."

"I can't make sense of you, Jinni. You grow hot and then cold without warning. Yes, of course. By all means, return to the lamp. Here is my wish: I ask health and long life and protection from harm for Barra."

"How long is long?" Jinni asked, his voice mulish. "As long as a tree? As long as a gnat? As long as a camel? As long as a—"

"As long as a mother should live!" cried Aminah. "To see her great-grandchildren born—and grow up!"

With another snap of his fingers, Jinni disappeared.

☽

PRINCESS BADR AL-BUDUR FOLLOWED Captain Saladin down a steep flight of steps carved out of the solid rock. The wide shaft wound down into the earth, curving out of sight, and was lit by oil lamps recessed in the walls. Two eunuchs clad in golden robes, their dark skin glistening in the lamplight, trailed behind the Full Moon of Full Moons.

"I've only heard of this place," said Badr, her voice hushed. "Father never brought me to see it, not that I cared until now."

"There is quite a network of rooms under the palace," Saladin said over his shoulder. "But of course, you speak of the dungeon."

They reached the foot of the stairway. A corridor ran left and right, and without hesitating, Saladin turned right. A minute or two later, they came to an iron door. The Captain of the Guard pounded his fist twice against the ironwork, and a face appeared in a high, narrow window, followed by loud rattling, muffled cursing, and then a resounding thump.

The door creaked open, revealing several prison guards who, upon seeing the Princess, salaamed. They stayed in their deep bows without moving, hands against foreheads, until Badr wondered if they'd turned to stone.

She was tempted to see how long the men could hold their positions, but Saladin's knowing smile irritated her. "Enough," she said, waving a hand in dismissal.

"Pardon the delay in opening the door, oh resplendent one," said the guard who had peered through the window. "The bolt is stubborn."

"Then clean off the rust," Saladin said, in a commanding tone. "But first, take us to the girls."

Badr lost track of the corridors and stairways that led deeper into the dungeon. The air was foul and filled with the faint rustling of vermin. She put a perfumed handkerchief to her nose and hurried after Saladin, who followed the guard through the murky passageways. Now and then a distant scream punctuated the grim silence. Each time Badr resisted the urge to glance back to make sure her faithful eunuchs were still close.

At last, the guard stopped at another iron door. It swung

open with ease, and Saladin ushered Badr into a small room. Two more guards salaamed, but their Captain pushed past them without a word and disappeared through yet another doorway.

The Princess ignored the guards as well, following Saladin into a long room ripe with the stench of urine. In the flickering lamplight, she saw a dozen beggar girls chained to the wall. Some of them were slumped in heaps on the cold stone floor. Others were hanging upright, wrists caught in manacles that dropped from the ceiling.

Badr drew close and was met by hollow stares, wide and white with terror. She surveyed the girls and saw blackened eyes and bloodied lips. Two of them lay unconscious, twisted and broken fingers cradled against their chests in silent agony. She stared at the girls' ruined hands, unable to pull her eyes away as an odd tingling sensation traveled across her midriff—a mixture of horror and pleasure.

"I had hoped to spare you this," said Saladin.

Though he didn't intend it, the gentleness in his voice mocked the broken figures lining the room. *Gentleness in such a place of brutality,* thought Badr, stifling a sudden, macabre need to laugh.

"Some of these girls are named Aminah. Some were found spending sums too large for a beggar. And others were caught trying to sell stolen lamps. But none has confessed to stealing *your* lamp, oh Full Moon of Full Moons, though I was very persuasive."

"They are smart enough to know that a confession means death," said Badr.

"Do you recognize any of them?" asked Saladin.

Badr had already scrutinized each girl and knew that her particular Aminah was not among them. Still, she said, "You've battered their faces beyond recognition. I would have thought a Captain of the Guard would know better."

Saladin smiled. "My mistake, dear Princess. I assumed I would find the girl without needing to involve you. However, I sense you are quite certain the thief is not here."

Badr felt another brief flicker of irritation. This man understood her too well for his own good. "I expect better results next time you drag me down here. Release these girls. They are of no use."

"Yes, oh effulgent one. My only purpose is to serve you."

Once the room was cleared, the princess turned to leave as well, then stopped. She stood still, thinking, then ordered her eunuchs to wait in the outer room. When they were gone, she drew near Saladin and took his hand. The iron face melted.

"Don't let the trail grow cold," she said, aware of the effect her touch was having on him. She released his hand and stepped away. "Next time, burn them with hot irons. It's very effective, I hear. But stay away from their faces."

Third Moon

· Eleven ·

AS SHE ANTICIPATED her third wishing moon, Aminah's
nightmares surfaced only infrequently, and then they were less
vivid and terrifying. Instead of dreaming, she often lay awake
mulling over what she'd learned from Talib and Hasim, and a
plan for how best to use her good fortune began to take shape
in her head.

While she waited for the moon, Aminah surprised Idris
with new warmth that made him suspicious.

"If I didn't feel so good, I'd think I was dying," he said. "I
can't imagine another reason you'd be so nice to me."

Aminah laughed and kissed his cheek, leaving Idris more
confused than before.

Barra noticed a change in her as well. Aminah was wont to
throw her arms around the cook and hug her fiercely. She
spent more time helping in the kitchen and the gardens. But
Barra was most surprised by a drop in the number of her visits to the suq.

Aminah also didn't miss a chance to join Idris and Barra on
the terrace in the evenings, where she taught them to find the
constellations as her father had once taught her. Sometimes
they played backgammon or moved to the garden for a game
of balls and mallets. Often she accompanied Idris on forays
into the desert, astride their stallions. But she also spent time
alone, reading and planning her next visit with Jinni.

Aminah also spent part of each day working in secret on a

project for Badr al-Budur. More than a month had passed since the royal witch had lost the lamp. If Aminah was right in assuming that the Princess knew about the jinni, then she also had to assume that Badr's patience and her temper were brittle by now.

Rather than just waiting and worrying, Aminah took action. She scoured the suqs until she found a lamp the mirror image of Jinni's. She bought engraving tools and practiced on other bits of brass until she could replicate the star with precision. She aged the decoy with salt water and sunshine, and then left it among a brass merchant's collection for the Sultan's guards to find.

The day after the decoy was planted, the full moon lifted above the rooftops, and Aminah wasted no time retrieving the real lamp from its hiding place. She gave it a brisk rub, but nothing happened. She stroked it harder, until her hand grew warm against its surface and the demon was forced out. He seeped reluctantly from the spout, materializing before her.

"Ask whatsoever thou desireth," he mumbled, careful not to look her way.

"You're still angry," said Aminah.

"Ask whatsoever thou desireth," Jinni repeated.

"You'd better tell me what's wrong," she said.

"Ask whatso—"

"I mean it!" Aminah cried, stamping her foot.

Jinni looked up, his eyes narrowing. "For an entire lunar cycle I waited, believing you intended to challenge me to a game of chess. After all, why else would you ask if I played? You summoned me and yet did not invite me to sit at the board."

"I should have asked you to play last time, but I was so tired from all my traveling—and throwing up. And after that night, I'd used up my wishes."

His face hardened. "Of course, Miss. No wishes, no need for Jinni."

"No, that's not it at all," Aminah said. "I didn't know you could be summoned until the next full moon—until I had wishes again."

Jinni's expression didn't change.

"And I didn't think you cared to play games with humans. You act like you hate every one of us."

"Indeed," said Jinni. "And you have reinforced my opinion."

"But I'd love to play chess with you," said Aminah.

"You are like all the rest. You are deceitful and selfish and—what did you say?"

"Let's play chess. Right now."

Jinni's look was blank. "Now?"

Aminah nodded. "I'll make a wish first, and then I'll teach you a lesson you won't forget. You're brave, Jinni, to challenge the likes of me."

"I *am* out of practice," Jinni mumbled.

Aminah laughed. "No excuses."

The demon puffed himself up, his body flaming with purple fire, though he couldn't hide the smile on his lips. "Insolence! I relish the thought of destroying you—harrying you from one corner of the board to another. Teach me a lesson? Ha! Get on with your wishes. Quickly!"

"If you're to become my chess partner, then you'll need a disguise," said Aminah. "I can't have you sitting around looking like . . . like a demon. What if Idris or Barra were to see you?"

Jinni stopped mid-bluster and cocked his head.

"If you're like my father, you'll want to play outside, under the trees by the fountain."

Jinni's eyes burned with anticipated pleasure. "The evenings are pleasant," he said.

"I can tell them you're my long-lost uncle, who'll be visiting from time to time. Can you make yourself look human?"

As Aminah watched, Jinni molded and rearranged himself as if he were made of clay. The result was a genuine human complexion and size. His attire had changed, too—wide trousers with a bright sash, a loose-fitting shirt, a vest, pointed shoes, a red-and-gold-striped jubba, and a black, high-peaked hat. He looked like a successful merchant—but a very young one.

She stared at him, surprised at his handsome features, and suddenly felt uncomfortable. "A little older," she said. "You look more like my long-lost brother."

This time there was a brilliant flash of damson-colored light, and before her stood a more mature version of the young man—still handsome but graying at the temples.

Her discomfort vanished, replaced by the odd sensation that she had seen this face before. She stared at Jinni, dredging her memories without success.

"You'll need a name," she said at last. "Something to give Idris and Barra."

Jinni bowed.

"Talib, perhaps. Or Hasim," said Aminah, smiling at her own cleverness. "Or Omar—"

Her father's name had escaped unbidden from her lips, and she stepped back, breathless. She could see it now—in the eyes, the shape of the nose. There was a hint of her father in Jinni's features.

"Let's call you Omar," she whispered.

Jinni didn't seem to notice the shocked expression on Aminah's face. He bowed again and said, "As you wish."

"Wait! That's *not* a wish."

"As you wish," he said.

"I do *not* wish!" she cried. "Stop doing that to me."

A deep laugh rumbled from Jinni—as warm as it was unexpected.

Aminah continued to stare at her father's face, flustered. "Well, then . . . I'm glad that's straightened out."

"Shall we proceed with your *real* wishes, Miss?" Jinni asked.

"Yes. Good. I was just about to suggest that." Aminah paused. "Say, can you grant wishes looking so . . . so human?"

Jinni rolled his eyes. "Appearance has nothing to do with it. I am the Slave between thy hands. Say whatso—"

Aminah held up a hand to stop him, then turned to gaze out her latticed window at the moon. "Jinni, I've had a lot of time to think since my last wishes. I want to do some good in the world, and I want you to help me."

"Jinn do not do good deeds. We are selfish," he said. "It is our nature."

"But I need your help. There's an old saying: 'One hand does not clap.' I can't do this alone."

"I must do as you command, but beware."

"Beware? What do you mean?" asked Aminah.

"Ah, nothing really. Only that I am not used to good deeds. Who can guess what might happen? There is another old saying you should know: 'If you see a lion's teeth, do not take it for a smile.'"

Aminah blinked. "You're talking in riddles. Will you help me or not?"

"I will help as you command me to help, Miss."

"Thank you . . . I think," she said, searching Jinni's eyes. He stared straight ahead.

Aminah sighed. "All right, I understand the wish-making rules," she continued. "I can't fix the whole world, but how about fixing a life here and there? I'll pick people who have good hearts, ones who will take what I've . . . what we've done for them and use it to help others."

"This will not work," said Jinni.

"Oh yes, it will. I saw it work on the road to Makkah, though it took me much too long to figure out what was happening. I have only three wishes a month, but if I choose the right people to help, then I can help hundreds, maybe thousands, in an indirect way."

"And how will you find the right people?" asked Jinni.

"My first wish, that's how. I need a seeing glass—a crystal ball or a magic mirror. Something that can show me any place, any time. That way I can find them."

"Do not forget that the gentle Princess is on your heels. Perhaps it is an army you need, rather than a scrying stone."

"I haven't forgotten, but I've taken care of her, at least for the time being." Jinni's eyebrows shot up in curiosity, but Aminah went on. "Stop trying to distract me," she said. "I wish for a seeing glass, and that's that."

A strange look settled on Jinni's face. "Granting wishes has become painfully boring, Miss, even the difficult ones," he said, stroking his beard. "It is the same thing decade after decade: gold, beauty, a bigger palace than the next fellow's—or even magic powers. But never good deeds for strangers. No one, in all my time, has bothered to help anybody else. This, at least, may be . . . interesting, especially when you have trouble finding a decent human being. Or when you find whom you think is the right sort but soon discover that he ends up smitten by greed or tempted by power. It should be quite entertaining."

"Entertaining?" Aminah eyed him suspiciously. "You won't turn my wishes sour somehow, will you?"

"It will not be necessary. Your humans will turn them sour on their own," said Jinni. "Now, as for your wish—"

He waved his arms in a crossing motion. With a loud snap and a puff of smoke, he was gone. In his place, cradled in a golden cup, sat a smooth orb of clear crystal, sparkling like a great diamond.

"Chess, Jinni! Did you forget? Come back!" Aminah started toward the lamp, which suddenly lurched out of her reach. It rattled and burped as she tried to grab it, but each time she got close, it hopped away. Then the lamp shot across the room, careening off walls and wooden chests, flipping spout over handle, and spinning like a top. It smashed two vases and a flowerpot before Aminah picked up a floor cushion and pounced, smothering the bronze dart as it flew by. When she got the lamp in her grasp, it squirmed and wriggled as if it were a living thing, but she held on and rubbed. The spout puckered, drew in air, and then spat out Jinni like a watermelon seed.

"By the seal ring of Solomon!" he cried. "Have I escaped the clutches of Azráeel?"

It looked as if Jinni had, indeed, brawled with the Angel of Death. His beard stood on end. His hat was backward. His new clothing was rumpled and torn. His sash wrapped around his neck like a hangman's noose, and he seemed to have been burned black. Acrid smoke rose from his body.

"Baked jinni!" said Aminah, trying hard not to laugh. "What happened?"

"I let myself be sucked into the lamp without thinking small. It is like stuffing a camel through a keyhole. The friction can set you aflame! Not pleasant, I tell you. Not pleasant at all."

"No, I wouldn't think so," said Aminah. "Why don't you straighten yourself while I straighten the room. Your lamp made a terrible mess—it even knocked over the chessboard."

Jinni snapped his fingers. He and the room were put to rights in the blink of an eye. "I clean up after myself," he said. "Now, Miss, to the chessboard. Prepare to be vanquished!"

· Twelve ·

ALONE at the end of the following day, Aminah curled up on her diwan. Her thoughts were on last night's chess game. It had been like playing against Omar—the real Omar—and though the match had been wonderful in its own way, it had also been unsettling. Jinni's new face would take some getting used to.

Moonbeams filtered through the window lattices, spattering the room with creamy patterns of light. As she sat, enveloped in the pale darkness, Aminah decided it was time to put her plan into action, and so she cleared her mind.

She cradled the orb in her palms, and images flickered into view. But the globe proved uncontrollable, scenes shifting with such speed she had less than a second to focus on anything. And the glass was clouded with veils of red smoke. Through the haze, she spotted fleeting faces and figures; but without a steady, clear picture, her search was impossible.

After two hours, Aminah threw the orb onto her bed, stamping her foot in frustration. She picked it up again, staring into its murky depths. *Worthless scrap of rubbish,* she thought, giving it a thorough shaking.

The orb grew dark red, then without any other warning, it exploded. Aminah screamed. Glass shredded her palms and fingers, blood gushing from a dozen deep cuts. She held out her hands as she ran from the room.

She hadn't taken two steps, when the pain stopped. Aminah stared at her hands—not a scratch, not a drop of blood. She turned back to the shattered orb. It lay nestled on a pillow—in one piece and filled with Jinni's leering face.

"One of my better illusions," he said, snickering. "Did you like it?"

"No," she answered, her voice trembling. "It was awful. *You're* awful!"

Jinni looked astounded. "You did not find it humorous?"

"If that's jinni humor, I don't think much of it. Bleeding to death isn't funny. And it hurt!"

His face clouded. "I meant no harm."

Aminah searched his eyes and then glanced at her hands again. "And no harm done, I suppose," she said. "But don't do anything like that again or . . . or I'll command you to run naked through the suq. Or I'll pour boiling water down the lamp's spout. Or I'll—what are you doing in my orb?"

"First of all, it is *not* your orb," said Jinni, his voice testy. "And second, have some respect for magic. Take care, Miss. Mystical devices are not merely objects. They have feelings. You called the orb worthless rubbish. You threw it, shook it. Offend the crystal, and it may sulk for months—perhaps years. Then it would be of no use to you."

"A sulking orb?" Aminah shook her head in wonder. "I'm surprised you stopped me and missed another laugh at my expense." She paused, seeing her father's eyes in the glass, and smiled. "I really do think you like me, Jinni."

"That has nothing to do with it. I stopped you to protect myself—purely selfish motives, I guarantee you," he said, lowering his voice. "The orb is on loan from a wizard with frightening powers. What if it were to go into a three-century sulk? I would be held responsible. Well, I will not have it!"

"This isn't my fault. You were too close-tongued—not telling me how it works. You never explain anything."

"Ask, and perhaps I will explain. I believe I have suggested this approach to you once before."

"Will it be at the cost of a wish?"

"Possibly."

Aminah threw up her hands. "By the way, I didn't call the orb a name. I only thought it."

"You are dabbling in magic. Thoughts are powerful. Use your thoughts to unite with the spirit of the orb, *not* to insult it." With that, he was gone.

Aminah sat down, taking the weight off her unsteady legs, and considered Jinni's advice. Then she took up the crystal and called out to it with her thoughts. Nothing happened at first, but then she began to sense a presence lurking at the edge of her consciousness. It was wary of her, and to lure it out, she tried begging its forgiveness. But the moment she spoke aloud, whatever it was disappeared.

For several hours, Aminah coaxed the spirit to come forth. Without using her voice, she called herself bad mannered and insensitive and begged its pardon again and again. She promised to be respectful, to be gentle. When nothing worked, she decided the crystal didn't trust her because it didn't know her, and so in great detail, she told it her life story. At last, she explained why she'd asked Jinni for the orb and pleaded with the spirit to help her.

As Aminah sent out her thoughts, she sensed the spirit watching her, peering around unseen corners, just out of sight somewhere in the red mists. Still, it wouldn't come to her.

Late in the night, Aminah fell exhausted onto her bed and

slept, the orb resting in her hand. Her dreams were like dervishes, twirling and winding in a meaningless jumble, and she was awakened more than once—or so she thought—to hear the rustling of leaves stirred by night breezes or the fluttering of finch wings against the wicker bars of their cage. The moon, rising to its apex, now shone with a cold, blue light, replacing the cream-colored arabesques with icy designs that appeared to ripple and dance across the carpeted floor. The mosaic patterns on her walls seemed to rearrange themselves into hideous faces, then angelic ones. She was never certain whether she was awake or asleep, never certain what was dream or reality, but she sensed that the orb held her in this strange place, somewhere in between consciousness and unconsciousness.

In the early morning hours, she felt a tentative presence step into the farthest reaches of her mind, where she harbored her darkest thoughts and her secret desires. Her instinctive reaction was to bar the way, to stop this worm from burrowing deep into her being. Instead, Aminah fought the urge, knowing the slightest resistance would drive the presence away and her chance with the orb would end.

Though not fully awake, she somehow was able to make a decision, allowing the crystal to sift her memories, to discover her inner self. It would know her better than anyone could, and then perhaps it would trust her.

She awakened at last to sun streaming through the carved window lattices. The orb was still in her grasp and felt as if it belonged there. She had opened herself to it, and now she knew it would open itself to her.

Aminah rose from her bed, clutching the orb to her breast.

It grew warm, and she felt rather than heard the spirit inside whisper a greeting. She answered, and a brilliant beam of red light flashed from the seeing glass. Then her stomach rumbled, reminding her how little she'd eaten the day before, and she set the globe on its golden stand. "I'll be back soon," she said.

Aminah entered the kitchen to find Idris and Barra. "We waited as long as we could," said Idris, "but I'm afraid we ate without you. Barra wondered if you'd died in your sleep!"

Barra laughed. "A young girl needs her sleep—to preserve her beauty. Look! I think it has worked well."

Idris's eyes wandered over Aminah and his look softened. "Yes, I believe you're right, Barra."

Aminah started to blush, but then Idris snorted. "But that's no excuse to lie around instead of making yourself useful," he said. "Why, I've exercised both horses already this morning."

"As if that's work," said Aminah. "Thank you, Barra." She gave the woman a quick hug. "As for Idris, I think living with the horses has given him the manners of a donkey."

Idris grinned, reaching for her hand. She let him take it.

"We should go for a ride, don't you think?" he asked, tracing her palm with his fingertip.

"I didn't know donkeys could ride horses," she said, color rising in her cheeks again.

"I'm only an ass by day," said Idris. "So we'll ride at sunset. What do you say?"

Aminah laughed, pulling her hand away to accept the food Barra was offering. "If I'm up from my afternoon nap."

"No nap," said Barra. "This afternoon we visit the suq. I need your help choosing flowers for the garden."

She couldn't resist an outing with Barra—and Idris, who insisted on coming along. After the dishes were cleared and washed, she hastened to change her clothes, apologizing to the crystal as she left. To her relief, it seemed to understand and whispered a cheery good-bye.

The orb was patient with Aminah's sunset ride, too. She and Idris circled the entire city and then galloped to the rock outcropping near where she'd hidden the ducats. Atop the hill, they rested their mounts, the evening breezes cooling the animals' heaving flanks.

"Do you ever feel guilty that we live so well?" Aminah asked Idris, as they sat looking down on the night-shrouded city.

Idris looked at her in surprise. "Why? I'm happier than I've ever been. For that I should feel guilty?"

Aminah shrugged. "There's so much misery in Al-Kal'as."

Idris was silent. "Yes," he said at last, lacing his fingers through hers. "But not in our home. Thank you, Zubaydah. I haven't said that often enough." He leaned in to kiss her.

Aminah turned her face so his lips brushed her cheek, and then she squeezed his hand. "We'd better get back," she said.

☽

WHEN SHE RETURNED to her rooms, Aminah went straight for the orb, in part to keep her mind off Idris. It was impossible to untangle the mixed-up emotions of the day. When had this happened between them—these feelings? But she sensed that things were going in the wrong direction. Of course, she loved him—in the same way she loved Barra. What if he expected more than that? She couldn't give more, especially not now that the orb was ready for the work to begin.

She cradled the crystal in both hands, and it grew warm

to the touch, almost hot. She sat without moving, in tense anticipation of what was about to happen. Then she felt the very essence of her life begin to flow into the orb. A remote part of her mind suggested this ought to frighten her, but it didn't. Instead, her heart swelled with delight until it felt near bursting.

Suddenly, the energy taken from her returned in a mighty rush. Her mind became the orb, the orb her mind. Then the crystal cleared, and together they began the search for the right sort of person to accept Aminah's help.

The orb's spirit understood her fear of Badr al-Budur, so it took them away from Al-Kal'as. It also understood Aminah's mission and was soon scanning some other great city—probing minds, measuring hearts, testing souls. Aminah watched images flash across the crystal with blinding speed, only now she had the power to see each one clearly—and to feel the love and anguish, the hate and joy in each heart.

Aminah was lulled by the jumble of sights and sounds, so when the orb froze on a single image, she was caught by surprise. The crystal was locked onto a large, run-down building. A sagging sign above the door announced that this was the shop of Ahab, THE FINEST TAILOR IN DAMASCUS.

Before Aminah could think of what to do next, the tailor's door opened and a well-dressed man stepped into the street.

"The zakah is overdue, Ahab," the man shouted into the dark recesses of the shop. "And the Sultan's special tax, too. The Master of Taxes has been patient. I have been patient. But no longer. You will pull the money together by month's end, or we must sell your needles, your thread, your cloth . . . your shop, if necessary."

Ahab the tailor stumbled to the door. He clutched at his thin beard with long, nimble fingers. "No, please. Let me pay a little now, a little each month. Think of my children."

The tax collector laughed, as three small heads peered around Ahab's legs. "*Your* children! A collection of orphans, beggars, and street urchins!"

Aminah caught her breath.

"You can't feed yourself," he continued. "You can't pay your taxes. A widower the likes of you has no business collecting children."

"They need me," the tailor replied.

"And the Sultan needs your taxes. Month's end, Ahab. Or you'll be a street urchin yourself."

Ahab watched the tax collector until he disappeared around the corner, then leaned his tall, gaunt frame against the doorpost. "Sharifah," he said, his eyes turned heavenward. "Why did you leave me? I need you to help me think."

Then he straightened and gently untangled himself from the eight little bodies that had come to crowd around him. "Oh Allah, what am I to do?" he asked, as he closed the door.

The image in the orb changed to show the inside of Ahab's shop. Twelve children stood about with grim faces. The three smallest, two little girls and a boy, still clung to Ahab's legs.

The tailor smiled and put his arm around the tallest boy, who seemed to be twelve or thirteen. "Don't worry. Now that I've taught Antar to help me measure and cut the fabric, we can work faster. We'll soon have enough for the zakah, and then perhaps the Master of Taxes will give us more time to pay the rest."

Antar shook his head but kept quiet.

"I know what you're thinking, Antar," said Ahab. "You're thinking that working faster won't help if we don't have customers. But I have a plan to attract new customers . . ."

His voice and image faded, and Aminah sat back against her pillows. While she'd watched and listened to Ahab, the orb had also shown her his heart. This tailor cared more for the children he'd picked up off the streets than he cared for himself. His was as kind a heart as she would ever encounter. But Aminah also knew that he didn't have a plan, though he was twisting his brains to come up with one.

Don't worry, Ahab, she thought. *I have a plan for you.*

❯

IN THE MORNING, Aminah found Idris in the kitchen with Barra. He smiled when she entered, but she could tell he was ill at ease. He fidgeted with the utensils and moved his food about on his plate until she reached over and patted his hand. He smiled again—almost a sad smile, she thought—and then the conversation picked up. It was as if a curtain had lifted, and soon the three of them were laughing and joking with one another in usual fashion.

That afternoon, they planted flowers together—the plants they'd acquired the day before in the suq. It was clear that Barra was skilled with flower gardens as she guided her young charges through the proper procedures for bedding roses— white ones were Barra's personal favorites. Then they planted violets, irises, gillyflowers, jasmine, and poppies. Aminah especially loved the violets.

They worked until evening shadows reached out to touch the petals. After a quick supper, Idris and Aminah were still so giddy from the mingling of intoxicating scents that Barra sent them to their rooms to recover. But instead of resting, Aminah changed her clothes and took up the orb, asking it to show her Ahab's shop. With the place fixed in her mind, she closed her eyes and imagined herself there, standing in the middle of the tailor's workroom.

She dropped into the shop and landed with a loud thump in a wooden bucket hidden in the shadows. With her left foot stuck in the bottom, Aminah clumped forward.

The tailor, sitting at his worktable, yelped and fell backward off his stool. The vest he was stitching flew in the air as his head struck the floor.

"Ahab!" Aminah cried, kicking the bucket loose. It flew across the room, narrowly missing the man's face.

Stunned, Ahab struggled to sit up before she could reach him and then cowered before her. "Allah, deliver me!" he said, raising his arms.

The older children poured into the room and ran to their foster father, helping him stand. Aminah backed away.

"Begone, demon!" Ahab pointed a shaking finger at her.

Now Aminah was stunned. How could this have gone so wrong? "No, you don't understand . . ." she began, ducking as the children pelted her with anything in reach. She dodged spools of thread, a measuring stick, a brass lamp, and the same bucket she'd kicked from her foot. But when Antar reached for a long, curved knife, she shut her eyes and imagined home.

Aminah could still feel the wind from the passing knife as she materialized in her chambers—and her cheek tingled. But all she found was a nick in her veil, and she collapsed on the diwan in relief.

Instead of going back for another try, Aminah summoned Jinni for a game of chess, hoping it would settle her nerves. But when Jinni found out Ahab had mistaken her for a demon, he laughed so hard that he lost control and was sucked back into the lamp. "Thinking small. Thinking small," she heard him cry as he disappeared.

At first Aminah's face burned with humiliation, but then she was so surprised by his laughter—deep, melodious belly laughs rising from the spout—that she laughed, too.

She waited until the lamp was silent, then called Jinni back. He appeared, looking the part of Omar. "Your uncle, Miss, at your service," he said, and then burst into laughter again.

"Stop it!" said Aminah, trying to look stern.

"Is that a wish?" Jinni asked.

"No, it's not a wish."

"Good," he said, laughing harder.

"We can't play chess if you're braying like a donkey. Besides, Idris will hear you and come running."

"No one can hear me but you, Miss, unless I allow it, and even then it is not very loud. Have you forgotten?" He forced a straight face. "No one would hear me, even if I were stomping about with a bucket on my foot."

Aminah turned in surprise. "How do you know about that?"

"Instant replay, Miss." Jinni snickered.

"*Instant replay?* What does that mean?"

He pointed to the orb, which was showing her moments with Ahab over and over. She could feel its laughter, too, as the crystal filled with festive wisps of scarlet smoke. Aminah's face grew warm. She *did* look ridiculous.

"What were you hoping to accomplish, Miss? Amputation? Suicide?"

"I was trying to help Ahab," Aminah said, feeling peevish now. "He's going to lose his shop if we don't do something. Then what will happen to his orphans? I know you don't care about orphans, Jinni, but I do. I know what it feels like to be one."

"As for orphans," said Jinni, sounding peevish himself, "I have nothing against them in particular—I possess an equal dislike for everyone. It is a demon's lot."

"You keep telling me that," said Aminah, "and I still don't believe you. What about Ahab? I need to talk to him before making wishes, but he'll run the second I appear. Or skewer me with sharp objects."

"Enter his shop as a customer."

"Of course!" Aminah clapped her hands. "It worked with Hasim, so why not with Ahab? You're brilliant, Jinni!"

"I was *not* trying to be helpful," he said. "I spoke without thinking."

Aminah smiled. "Whatever you say."

"Beware! A jinni's counsel may lead to destruction." He put on a fierce purple face, eyes flashing fire.

"You're slipping," said Aminah. "I've seen uglier faces on the Sultan's guards. The rear end of a camel is scarier."

Snakes leapt from his mouth and ears. His head spun around on his shoulders, and when it stopped, his eyes fell from his head and rolled on the floor. Blood oozed from his nose and empty eye sockets.

"Ooh, much better," she said. "By the way, thanks for the warning."

"For the last time, I do not give . . ." Jinni sighed. "Never mind. Are we playing chess, or do I return to my brass prison?"

"The snakes were a nice touch," said Aminah, as she watched another wriggle from Jinni's mouth, "but get rid of them, please. Then get a new face and meet me at the chessboard."

The game lasted only an hour. Aminah couldn't concentrate, and Jinni won with little effort. He gloated, making biting comments about the inferior intellect of humans and snickering with devilish delight.

"I suppose being an ungracious winner is a demon's lot, too," said Aminah.

Jinni smiled and nodded, then began slipping into the lamp. Before his head disappeared, he paused, catching Aminah's eye.

"Thank you, Miss."

· Thirteen ·

EARLY THE NEXT MORNING, there was a knock at Aminah's door. She stirred, sitting up in bed only to fall back, moaning. Her head throbbed, and when she tried opening her eyes, the stinging pain caused her to cry out.

Aminah covered herself and then stumbled to the door, squinting through one eye to find her way. Unable to face the sunlight, she unlatched it and turned away.

Idris peered into a room darkened by shaded windows.

"Shut the door! It's too bright."

Idris spotted Aminah sprawled on the diwan, scratching at herself. Then she turned to look at him, and Idris gasped. Her face was no more than a swollen lump—slits for eyes, a nose lost inside bulbous flesh.

Idris shouted for Barra. She was in the room within seconds and had no more than glanced at Aminah before she ran back the way she came. "Don't let her scratch anymore!" Barra yelled over her shoulder.

Idris grabbed Aminah's wrists. She struggled against his grip, twice trying to bite him. He was wondering how much longer he could last when Barra rushed back into the room, a large jar under her arm.

While Idris still held her, Barra tied thick cloth coverings on Aminah's hands. "Now get out of here," she ordered him. He seemed relieved to go.

It took all of Barra's strength to hold Aminah down and

undress her. Then she dipped her fingers into the jar and began slathering every inch of Aminah's body with yellowish salve the consistency of paste. Within moments, Aminah lay still, her rapid breathing settling back to normal. Soon, her facial features began to reappear as the swelling receded, but beneath the salve, her arms, legs, and torso were crisscrossed with long scratches.

Later, Barra let Idris back in the room to sit with a freshly clothed Aminah while she went to the suq to purchase the ingredients needed to concoct another batch of her miracle cure.

"Drink," he said, holding a glass of sherbet to her lips.

Aminah sipped the cool liquid. It eased the raw dryness in her throat.

"Well, that was a surprise," she said, smiling as she pushed the drink away. "And I don't mean the sherbet. What do you suppose happened to me?"

"Something you ate, I imagine."

"Perhaps. Though I don't think I ate anything I haven't eaten a hundred times before. Anyhow, thanks for rescuing me. And sorry I tried to bite you."

Idris shrugged. "It's Barra you should thank. I'm glad your real face is back. The other one required full-time veiling."

Aminah laughed. "Really? That bad?"

"Sorry," said Idris. "How's the headache?"

"Barra gave me a strong dose of some sort of foul-tasting powder. I'm feeling fine now."

"Hello, what's that?" Idris stood, starting across the room. Aminah felt sick again. She'd forgotten to put away the orb. "Where'd you get it?" he asked, reaching to take the crystal from its stand.

"Don't!" Aminah cried.

Idris jerked back his hand as if from a hornet's sting, throwing her a dark look. "More secrets?" he asked. "Like the secret visitor in your quarters last night? Perhaps this is a gift from him."

"Were you spying on me?" Aminah knew she should be indignant, but she couldn't muster the energy. She could tell from Idris's pained expression that he'd slipped—he hadn't intended to say anything about her mysterious guest. *He's jealous,* she thought.

"I assumed you finally trusted me," Idris said, in a low tone. "But that's ridiculous—you won't even give me your real name."

"You know I can't. We've been over this a hundred times. Don't bring it up again."

They stared defiantly at one another through the gloom.

"I only heard your voice, as I was passing by," he said, dropping his eyes. "The windows were shaded. Who were you talking to, Zubaydah?"

"Perhaps I was talking to myself."

"Part of my job is looking after you," he said. "Protecting you. How can I do that if you're sneaking around behind my back?"

Aminah felt the heat rise in her face. "I don't need your protection. And you don't need to know everything."

"I care about you, Zubaydah. Please."

Aminah sighed. "Someday I'll tell you more, I promise, but right now it's better if I don't."

"I just hope your secrets don't get us killed," said Idris.

"What do you mean?"

"Someone was watching the house. I kept meeting this fellow on the street. Sometimes he'd be in one of the alleys or standing in a doorway. When I started watching for him, he noticed and stopped coming. Now there's another fellow—"

"Why didn't you tell me?" she demanded.

"I thought it was a coincidence, or that I was being too suspicious," he said. "Clearly your secrets are something to worry about, and if you'd only warned me . . . but then, you don't need protecting. Or maybe you have another protector. One who guards you at night."

Aminah shook her head in disgust. "Don't worry if you hear me talking to myself," she said. "I'm not with anyone you need to worry about."

"So you are with someone."

"Yes—my finches."

Idris closed his eyes and stood still for a moment. "I hope you know what you're doing," he said.

"I do," Aminah answered. She paused, looking about the room, then reached out for a bright blue vase. "When I set this outside the door, I mustn't be disturbed. Or listened to, for that matter. Is that clear? I promise I'll be safe. Tell Barra."

"It's about more than just being safe," Idris said. "Oh, never mind. I'm leaving now."

"What about the people watching the house?" she asked as he pulled open the door.

"What do you want me to do?"

"Act like we suspect nothing, but keep watching. Don't be upset, Idris. You'll know everything soon enough."

He gave her a curt nod and was gone.

Aminah waited a few minutes and then set the blue vase

outside. She stripped off her clothes, rubbing more of Barra's salve on the angry rash that still speckled her armpits, her stomach, and the crooks of her arms and legs. The medicine made the itching bearable.

Unsettled by most everything Idris had said, Aminah didn't know what to think about first. What should she do about Jinni's nocturnal visits? Was the Princess watching her? And how should she handle Idris? It seemed she hadn't handled him well so far.

And, of course, she couldn't ignore her ballooning face, splitting headache, and torturous rash. What was behind it all? The answer became clear a moment later when she picked up the orb to put it away inside the hidden room. As her fingers brushed the crystal, pain pierced her skull like an arrow, and beneath the salve, the rash boiled. Aminah retreated, and the pain lessened slightly.

Irritation turned to fury as she retrieved the lamp and summoned Jinni. He drifted from the spout and was assaulted by an angry fist waving in his face.

"You're a lout. A giant, demonic lout! And I was foolish enough to think we were starting to be friends. You knew what linking with the orb would do to me. I'll wager you had a good laugh when my face swelled like a goat bladder. And look at this rash!" She pulled up her sleeve and thrust out her arm. "And the headache . . ." Aminah blanched and sat down, cradling her face in her hands. "Still hurts," she whispered.

No sound came from Jinni. She looked up and discovered he wasn't there. Aminah gave up on him and lay down with a pillow over her head, trying to ease the pain behind her eyes.

She hadn't been asleep long when a noise in the room

stirred her. She sat up, pushing the pillow aside, and saw Jinni standing next to her.

"How did you get here?" she asked, her voice slurred. "I thought you were in the lamp. I didn't call you out."

"I have not been in the lamp, Miss. I have been to see the wizard of the orb."

Aminah stared at him. "You didn't know this would happen, did you?"

"No, Miss. I would have enjoyed knowing, of course."

"And to think I was about to apologize for yelling at you."

"The wizard tells me that the first time is the most severe," said Jinni. "Your face will not swell again. The headaches will be minor in comparison."

"And the rash?"

"Unpredictable, but never again as serious."

"I suppose you didn't have to find this out for me, so I will apologize."

"That is decent of you," said Jinni. "May I have your leave to return to the lamp?"

"Look, I really am sorry. How about playing chess?" she asked.

"As you wish."

"It's not a wish, Jinni. I'll call for you later."

There was a faint smile on his lips as he disappeared.

Aminah set the blue vase back inside, and then she slept again, waking at Barra's touch.

"It's late afternoon," said Barra. "I brought you something to eat. Let me check the rash."

She was also carrying a fresh jar of salve, which she applied liberally as Aminah nibbled on dates and cheese. As there was still a dull ache in her head, Barra forced her to swallow more of the ill-flavored headache powder.

"The rash has almost cleared," she said, looking pleased with herself. "I wonder at the cause."

"Don't worry," said Aminah, squeezing Barra's hand. "If it comes again, I have a feeling it won't be as bad."

Barra's look was puzzled. "And how would you know such a thing?" she asked, but Idris tapped at the door, distracting her.

"I'm going out tonight, if no one objects," he said.

"Out riding?" asked Aminah.

Idris shook his head. "To meet some friends."

"You have friends in Al-Kal'as? I didn't know."

"You aren't the only one with secrets," he said.

Barra looked from Idris to Aminah and back to Idris. Aminah could tell she wanted to ask what was going on, but she kept quiet.

"No objections here," said Aminah. "Barra?"

"Of course not," said Barra. "Will you be here for supper?"

Idris shook his head. "I think I'll go now," he said, his eyes on Aminah.

"Have a good time," she said.

"That's my plan. See you tomorrow."

He stepped back through the door, but Aminah's voice stopped him. "Be careful, Idris."

◗

AS THE EVENING SHADOWS MERGED into darkness, Aminah set the vase at the door. She felt unsettled during the moments she was outside, as though aware of someone watching her. Maybe Idris had, indeed, seen the Princess's spies. Maybe the decoy hadn't been discovered, but Aminah had, and now a guard was waiting for the right moment to pounce. She hoped Idris wasn't angry enough with her to drop his guard, or worse . . .

Aminah shook her head and was relieved to feel no pain. She refused to become a prisoner in her own house. She had work to do, places and people to visit. Fortunately, she had a way to travel behind her closed door.

She washed the salve from her face and hands. She cleaned her teeth and chewed on mint leaves to freshen her breath. Then she changed her clothes for a trip to Damascus, dressing to hide her youth: layers of silk, heavy veils, and a dome-shaped cap with a circlet covered in pearls.

Finally, she retrieved the lamp. Though it should have been safe in the hidden room, Aminah was too nervous to leave it behind. She secured the lamp beneath her robes and then made the jump to Damascus. An image of the area around Ahab's shop was clear enough in her memory so that she didn't need the orb, much to her relief. Though she felt a genuine kinship with its spirit, she wasn't prepared for another rash.

The idea of materializing on the busy streets frightened her, however, so she chose the narrow alley running next to the shop. It had been deserted when the orb last showed the building. Still, she considered using the crystal to be certain there were no buckets hidden in the shadows. Instead, she made the leap on faith alone and arrived with both feet planted on the empty stretch of paving stones.

Straightening her cap, she stepped out into the street and headed for Ahab's shop. She paused at the door, rehearsing what to say, and then stepped inside.

Streaks of late-afternoon sunlight filtered through the latticed windows, but the shop was cool and dim. Ahab rose from his sewing table, his face registering surprise at Aminah's expensive clothing. All the children were out of sight, except for Antar, who knelt in a corner of the room measuring and marking cloth.

"*Sabah el khair,*" said Ahab, bowing.

"Yes, good morning," Aminah answered.

"How may I help you, Madam?"

"Thawb," Aminah said. She was nervous and her voice squeaked.

"You wish me to sew a thawb for you?" Ahab hurried to a shelf and lifted a large, flowing robe. "My work is very fine, Madam. My robes are ample, the sleeves wide. Would you like fine silk or purest linen?"

"Some . . . some of both. With images of birds, perhaps. And gold edging. Ten of your very best thawbs."

"Ten?" Ahab threw a joyous look at Antar. "But Madam, my best are very expensive—so much gold trim and embroidery. Each may cost as much as—"

"The price is not important," she said. "And I will pay you a thousand dinars in advance."

"Oh no, Madam!" Ahab waved his hand in the air, his eyes popping. "It is too much."

"For the best materials? For gold trim and embroidery? If your work is as good as I'm told, then a thousand is too little. If it comes to more, then I'll pay the rest when the robes are completed."

"Please, Madam. I cannot take so much in advance."

"I trust you. The thousand dinars are yours to keep, no matter what."

"But Madam—"

"When should I return for them? A month?"

He nodded.

Aminah leaned forward and whispered, "Pay your debts, Ahab. And if a visitor comes again in the night, don't throw knives at her."

Ahab's mouth fell open. Antar jumped up, backing away with fear in his eyes.

"May the blessings of Allah fall on your head, Ahab. You, too, Antar." She laughed at the shock on their faces. "A demon wouldn't call on our merciful Allah, would she?"

They shook their heads in unison.

"The robes in a month, then?"

"*Inshallah*," Ahab murmured.

"Yes, God willing," said Aminah.

· Fourteen ·

"HERE'S WHAT I WANT you to do, Jinni." Aminah stood with her arms crossed, a determined look on her face. "I want you to shrink yourself to the size of a mouse and ride in my pocket."

"This . . . this is an outrage!" Jinni cried, sputtering. "An outrage! An indignity!"

"A favor," she said. "Not a wish. Not a command. A favor for a friend."

"Jinn do not have friends." Ugly purple steam curled from his ears.

Aminah looked hurt. She picked up the black elephant from the chessboard, holding it up for Jinni to see. "Aren't we friends? We play chess together, plus you went to the wizard for me about the orb. Those are the marks of friendship."

His eyes traveled between the chess piece and her face. "Do not ask this of me," he said.

"But you can't grant wishes from inside the lamp. You said so yourself. And we don't want Ahab to see you. He's crazy when it comes to demons."

"Then make your wishes from here. You can travel between this house and Damascus in an instant. It will be as though you never left him."

"But it would be more fun," she said. "Imagine Ahab's face when I speak the wishes. Please, Jinni."

Jinni's resentment was opening a dark pit between them,

and Aminah quickly stepped away from the edge. "Forget I asked. It was a bad idea."

"May I return to the lamp?" he asked, his voice brittle.

Aminah nodded. "Did I hurt your feelings?" she asked.

"Jinn do not have feelings," he said, as he faded away.

She watched the last of his smoke stream down the spout before grabbing a pillow and hurling it across the room. Had she really expected a demon to ride in her pocket? She buried her face in her hands, ashamed that she'd tried to coerce Jinni by dangling a chess piece in front of him. She may as well have said, "You owe me this because I've been kind to you." But Aminah knew a slave owed a master nothing.

She crossed to the window and gazed into her garden. The moon's reflection shimmered in the fountain's pool, dancing to the measured beat of cricket music. She drew in a breath of jasmine-scented air and turned to look at the lamp, hoping she could set things right with Jinni.

This was the perfect time to introduce Idris and Barra to Uncle Omar, she decided. They would help smooth over the trouble. Idris could offer Omar a ride on the Arabians, if jinn rode horses. And Barra could feed him. Food was always a worthy peace offering. Then Aminah realized she'd never seen Jinni eat. He'd never asked for so much as a drink of water. Perhaps jinn didn't like food. Or couldn't eat at all.

When they sat across from one another at the chessboard, it often seemed like being with her father. But the moment wishing entered the picture, everything changed. She shook her head in frustration. How could she ever be expected to figure out a jinni? Ahab's confusion over her magical appearance couldn't have been much greater than what she was feeling now.

To get her mind off Jinni, she decided to look in on Ahab again. She was careful to dress the same as before so the tailor would recognize her. Then, concentrating on a bare stretch of floor inside his shop, she made the leap.

Ahab was alone when she appeared. His needle flashed in the lamplight, dancing in and out of a thawb the color of an ocean sunrise. Though Aminah's arrival was noiseless, a telltale puff of air stirred the tailor's beard, and he looked up.

"Madam," he said, standing. "I didn't expect you so soon. I am working on your first thawb. Do you like the color?"

"Yes," she answered. "I've seen it before. In the morning sky off the coast of Tyre."

Ahab pointed to the floor at her feet. "I keep that spot clear, now. For Allah's angel. Is that star on your forehead an angel's mark?"

Aminah smiled behind her veils, but she didn't correct him. She touched the scar, hoping Allah would forgive her silence. "Are your taxes paid?" she asked.

"Yes, Madam." Ahab scratched his beard. "Is it proper to call an angel Madam?"

"It is good enough for me," she said. "How are the children?"

"Magnificent! They feel safe again. I picked up a thirteenth today, you know. Her name is Zalikha. You should have seen her—skin and bones. But I'll fatten her up in no time."

Ahab stopped, his eyes misting, and he dropped to his knees. "Last time, I allowed you to leave without hearing a word of gratitude. How could I do that, Madam? I beg your forgiveness as I thank you. My children thank you also."

"You are welcome, Ahab," she said. "But you need to thank

yourself, as well. I'm here only because of what you're doing for Antar and the others."

He looked surprised. "I could not do otherwise. As the old saying goes, children are the wealth of the Arabs."

Aminah sniffed. "Not orphans, it seems. Ahab, you can do a lot more for these children. What would help? More money? Then, instead of working, you could spend your time rounding up all the Antars and Zalikhas."

Ahab shook his head. "I love being a tailor. Besides, the children need to see me work, don't you think? So if I just had plenty of customers . . ." He laughed. "And could sew a little better and a little faster."

"A bigger house?" she asked. "A newer shop?"

"No, Madam. You've given us enough."

"No, I haven't. Help me with this. There's nothing I can't do for you."

"Can you bring back my Sharifah?" he asked, then looked up at Aminah in horror. "Forgive me, Madam!"

"Your wife?" she asked, already knowing.

He nodded. "I shouldn't have said such a thing. Sometimes I act as if I'm an orphan, too."

"You're lonely," said Aminah, unbidden images of her mother's deep despair filling her head.

"It is true. Without my children, I couldn't go on." Ahab smiled. "But as it is, I am happy. The little ones bring me great joy."

Aminah blinked back unexpected tears. If only her mother had been as strong as Ahab—or Barra, for that matter. But then maybe it wasn't possible for everyone to be so strong.

"Ahab," she said, stifling a sniffle, "I'm not finished with you. Watch for miracles."

☽

BACK IN HER ROOMS, Aminah threw off the layers of clothing and pulled away the veils. She dressed in a light linen shift and sarwal, then crept from her quarters to find something cool to drink in the kitchen. As she crossed the courtyard, a dark figure stepped from the shadows and grabbed her arm. Moonlight glinted from a knife blade. She jerked free with a strangled yelp and started to run.

"Zubaydah!"

"Idris!" Aminah stopped, turning to face him. "Put that knife away, you idiot."

"Idiot? Who's the idiot?" he whispered, as the knife disappeared into his jubba. "You're the one who broke the rules."

"What are you talking about? The rule is: don't jump out at me with knives."

"The vase," said Idris. "It's still outside your door."

"Oh, the vase," she said, sounding cross.

"'Idris,' I asked myself, 'if Zubaydah is safe in her suite, who's that sneaking through the courtyard?'"

"I wasn't sneaking. And what if I'd been Barra? You might have slit her throat."

Idris shrugged. "Where are you going? It's late."

"This is my house. I can come and go as I please."

"But—"

"The kitchen, Idris. I was on my way to the kitchen. See, nothing dangerous, though I was thinking of taking a stroll in Beggars' Corridor afterward." Aminah started across the courtyard, leaving him behind.

"Very funny," Idris called out. "Go ahead, brush me aside—but at your own peril. Someone's watching you, Zubaydah. I'm sure now."

She stopped, turning to listen.

"I've spotted the same fellow a half-dozen times in the last two days, and I don't think he's here for Barra or me. Who's after you, Zubaydah? And why?"

"I don't know," Aminah said. "Perhaps he's nothing but a thief, waiting for the best opportunity."

Idris snorted in disgust. "I can't watch this place day and night, especially if I don't know what I'm up against."

"Then don't watch it. Tomorrow I'll hire a porter—no, two porters—to guard the gate. You'll be free of the worry, and I'll be safe."

"Free of the worry! You think that's all this is about? That I don't want the responsibility?"

"I thought hiring porters would make you happy," said Aminah. "I can't seem to win with you."

"Stop," he hissed, clenching his fists. In the darkness she heard the grinding of his teeth. "You're blind, Zubaydah. Blind and stubborn."

Idris stepped back, melting into the shadows. Aminah stared into the night, unnerved by the heat of his anger—and by how quickly he'd vanished. She'd felt so fortunate to find him, to have him in her life, but now . . . Had she been wise?

And what of Idris's revelation that spies were lurking outside? She still believed that if Badr had had the slightest suspicion, her guards already would have taken the house apart. But then who was watching her?

After a time, Aminah made her way to the kitchen and then

returned to her quarters with two banana-flavored sherbets. She left the vase where it was and barred her door. She sat on the diwan, sipping the cool, sweet water, and forced herself to concentrate on Ahab and the two wishes she'd saved for him.

Aminah knew she could make his business a success, but he needed something more. He needed someone to help him care for the children, someone to care for him. *Ahab needs Sharifah,* she thought.

She was sure Jinni's magic wasn't strong enough to raise the dead, but perhaps he could do the next best thing for Ahab. She took a long drink, then set her sherbet aside and rubbed the lamp.

Smoke streamed from the spout, and Jinni hovered before her, purple and grim. "Say whatso—"

"Jinni, forgive me."

The cloud that still trailed from his waist into the lamp slowly formed as legs, and in a moment Uncle Omar stood next to her.

"I didn't mean to insult you," said Aminah. "It was a stupid idea. And rude. I don't know what I was thinking to suggest such a thing."

"You are not angry with me?" Jinni asked.

Aminah shook her head. "I have a sherbet for you. Banana. Do you drink? Or eat? May I get you something else?"

"Jinn need no nourishment," he said, grabbing the sherbet from her fingers. "Yet we crave the tastes, the smells."

With a single tip of the glass, he emptied it, emerging with a wide smile. "Another first, Miss. No human, except you, has offered me refreshment. This is the only drink I have had since . . . I do not remember my last drink."

"You can't conjure a sherbet for yourself?"

"No," said Jinni. "We can only take in food and drink offered by human hands, which almost never happens. And, of course, we cannot ask."

"Who makes these silly rules?" asked Aminah.

Jinni looked over his shoulder. "Quiet, Miss," he whispered. "Do not anger the Powers."

"But—"

Jinni raised his hands, pleading for her to stop.

"Fine," she said. "But the Powers—whatever they are—can't stop me from feeding you. Count on it every time you visit. I'll serve you as if . . . as if you were my own father."

Jinni blinked. "As you wish, Miss."

Aminah sighed. "It's not a wish, Jinni."

"But it is your decision," he said. His tone was somber, but his face was celebrating. "Now, what may I do for you on this magnificent evening?"

"I took your advice, Jinni," she said, smiling at the hungry look on his face. "I visited Ahab during the day and paid him a thousand dinars to make ten thawbs for me."

"Now he can pay his taxes," said Jinni. He lifted the glass again, coaxing out another drop.

"Humans' lives can become knotted, you know, and seem hopeless. But every knot has someone to undo it," said Aminah. "We're about to undo Ahab's knot."

"Are you quoting the famous Talib again?" asked Jinni.

Aminah grinned. "Yes. And Talib was right—Ahab benefits not only himself but also others. He has thirteen orphans now. Thirteen! And if we help him to help himself from now on, he'll take in even more. Instead of thieves and beggars, they'll become tailors and merchants and scholars. Best of all, they'll follow Ahab's example. Kindness will breed kindness. This is exactly what I'd hoped for, Jinni."

"Then your plan is working," he said, eyeing her glass of sherbet.

"Here," said Aminah. "Have the rest of mine."

Jinni's face lit up. She waited until the second glass was empty and then said, "I want to use my last two wishes to ensure Ahab's future. Will you do your best for him?"

"Sherbet makes for a happier, more compliant jinni. So, yes, Miss, I will do my best."

☽

AFTER PAYING the zakah and the Sultan's special tax, Ahab had plenty of money left over. So the next day, after morning prayers, he sent Antar for tailoring supplies.

"And get something good for supper," he called, as the boy ran from the shop, gleeful at the prospect of spending two or three hours combing through the suq.

Ahab saw to it that the other children were settled at work or play and then started on the second of Aminah's thawbs. He pulled out the cloth, turquoise linen, and rubbed it between his fingers.

I wish it were a sky blue, he thought, then blinked his eyes in surprise. The fabric had become so much like the summer sky that he expected clouds to float across its surface.

"It must be the poor light in here," he said. "It seemed a different shade. As it is, the color is perfect, but perhaps a brocade would be better—a pattern of birds in flight."

No sooner had the words left his lips than the cloth stirred in his hands, and he felt the texture change as a pattern of swallows, wing tips touching, rose under his fingers. Ahab was about to bolt for the door when he remembered Aminah's last words: "Watch for miracles."

"Could this be?" he wondered aloud, and he decided to test his new power. Ahab set the cloth aside and said, "I do believe this would be better in silk." Nothing happened. Then he held the fabric and said the same thing. The material in his hands became silk—the finest, sky-blue, brocaded silk.

I need this an arm's span longer, he thought. Snakelike, the textile writhed and slithered forward as it lengthened.

Ahab hopped about his shop, hugging the piece of silk to his breast, then stopped as an idea struck him. He dropped the cloth, grabbing a bit of bread left from his breakfast.

"I wish this were a sweetmeat," he said, but the bread did not change. Then Ahab knelt to pick up the corner of a small rug. "I wish this were a room-sized carpet." Nothing happened.

He hurried back to the worktable and lifted his scissors. "I wish these were gold."

Nothing.

"I wish these were twice as long and twice as sharp."

With a groan, the metal elongated as a grinding noise pierced the air. Ahab touched the cutting edge and was left sucking a bleeding finger.

He continued to experiment, and soon it was plain that anything to do with tailoring was magic in his hands. Needles multiplied in his palm; thread became thicker or thinner or changed colors; fabrics rewove themselves. And the quality of every item surpassed the best the world had to offer.

Ahab sat, stunned at the possibilities. He picked up Aminah's first thawb and stitched as he planned for the future. He would sew the fabrics of kings, and perhaps kings would be among his patrons. Ahab smiled at the thought of a new house with a hundred rooms for hundreds of children. Then he looked down at his hands. They were flying across the thawb, many times faster than his fastest work. Every stitch was finer, tighter—better than his best sewing. He laughed and tried going even faster. His hands were a blur.

Ahab dropped the thawb and reached for the sky-blue piece of silk and his newly sharpened scissors. A daring new design for Aminah's next thawb leapt into his head, and he began to cut the cloth without marking it. The scissors sang as they sliced through the brocaded swallows, and in moments the garment was ready for stitching.

"A miracle," said Ahab, slipping from his stool to his knees.

He was still on the floor when the shop's door swung open. A woman's figure stood silhouetted against the sunlight. For a moment, he thought his angel had returned, but when she stepped inside, Ahab saw a woman older than Aminah.

"How may I be of service?" he asked, brushing the dust from his knees as he stood.

When she drew near, his eyes met hers and his heart leapt. He was peering into Sharifah's eyes! Ahab stepped forward, his breath coming hard, and studied the woman's face through her sheer hijab. She was not Sharifah, of course, and yet . . .

She gazed at Ahab, a strange look crossing her face. "Excuse me for staring, sir," she said. "I thought for a moment . . . But no, I've not been in this part of Damascus. I don't go out much, since my husband died. In fact, I'm uncertain what led me here today."

Her voice wasn't Sharifah's, but it was still like music. Forgetting propriety, he took her hand. She jumped at his touch but did not pull away.

"What is your name, Madam?"

"Khalidah," she answered, her fingers warm in his.

"And I am Ahab. Do you feel magic in the air?"

She nodded, looking about in awe.

The sound of scampering feet interrupted them, and Ahab turned to find thirteen pairs of eyes watching.

"Meet our children, Khalidah," he said.

She smiled and reached for his other hand.

☽

"LEAVE US." Badr al-Budur waved away her eunuchs. Their smooth, stony faces didn't so much as twitch. They passed Saladin and stationed themselves outside the doors to the Princess's apartment.

Once the eunuchs were gone, Badr turned on Saladin, her voice like a knife. "Two months! Two months, and you've nothing to show for it."

"I have arrested a hundred girls," said Saladin. "I have searched every suq, checking lamps by the thousands for the telltale star."

"Not that searching for the star did any good," she said, lifting Aminah's decoy from a shelf. "I rubbed this worthless piece of scrap until my fingers bled, all for nothing!"

"It fit the description, Princess. You said yourself it looked like Aladdin's lamp."

Badr dug her toes into the thick woolen carpet as if to keep herself from springing at the Captain of the Guard. She threw the lamp to the floor, clenching her fists and staring up at the carved, gold-flecked ceiling.

"Perhaps Aladdin lied to you," Saladin said.

"He didn't lie," she answered, her tone dangerous. "Nobody had ever heard of him before he appeared at our door draped in jewels. Isn't that strange for someone of his wealth and supposed station? It was plain to see that Aladdin was unfamiliar with riches. He was ill at ease with court life. Knew none of the courtly games. Had trouble controlling a spirited horse. Didn't even recognize half the dishes served at dinner. No, Aladdin came from nothing and would have been nothing but for the jinni of the lamp."

Saladin nodded. "Then we must at last consider the possibility that the lamp is no longer in Al-Kal'as. Or that it has been melted down to make some other brass trinket. If this beggar girl had rubbed the lamp, she either would have ridden out of the city on a magic carpet or would be living like the pharaohs of Egypt. I have no reports of a new resident who lives a life so lavish as to challenge that of yours. Still, I've ordered my men to canvass every home in Al-Kal'as, looking for the lamp, but there are many households, oh lustrous one. It will take time."

"We don't have time!" screamed Badr. She lashed out with her hand, raking Saladin's cheek and leaving a bloody trail.

The Captain of the Guard didn't flinch, but his eyes hardened and the look frightened the Princess. She threw aside her veil and collapsed against Saladin's chest. Then she stood on her toes to kiss the wound she'd inflicted on him. "Forgive me," she whispered in his ear.

Saladin put his arms around her. She let him hold her for a few seconds and then pulled away when she felt his body relax.

"The lamp is still in Al-Kal'as," she said. "I've told you that before and nothing's changed. It's here—I can feel it."

"Then the lamp's power remains undetected, which I find doubtful," said Saladin, "or it is in the hands of one who is cautious—cautious and disciplined. I have already posted spies in each neighborhood to watch for suspicious activity. I'll double their numbers."

"Triple them," said Badr. "Here's something you don't know yet, Saladin. My father's condition has worsened. He's dying, and he knows it. Today he sent a messenger to bring back Aladdin. I don't need to tell you what that means, do I?"

"No, Princess."

"I will not be denied what should be my birthright, Saladin. Without the lamp, no woman can be Sultan. Without the lamp, you will not be Grand Vizier or enjoy the intimate 'privileges' of that office. Will you be my Grand Vizier, Saladin?"

"Yes, Full Moon of Full Moons. No matter the cost, I will."

Fourth Moon

· Fifteen ·

"AHAB FINISHED them in days, not weeks," said Aminah, modeling a thawb of indescribable beauty. "This is number ten."

The thawb was red, but unlike any red she'd ever seen. And the pattern in the silk seemed alive—images changing, rearranging without warning. Camels lumbering across the desert became ships tossed on a wild sea, then falcons darting through the clouds.

Jinni lounged in front of the chessboard, sipping a yoghurt drink and nibbling from a tray of sweetmeats. It was the first day he'd been outside the lamp since he'd made Ahab a mystical tailor. Not that Aminah hadn't summoned him. She had a dozen times, but he'd been too weak to respond with anything more than a hollow voice speaking from the lamp's spout. Just as time travel and orb linking resulted in unexpected and unpleasant consequences for humans, so did good deeds for demons.

"Nothing to worry about," Aminah had called into the lamp. "I'm sure it will get easier each time."

Jinni hadn't answered her, and after two weeks, she'd begun to wonder if he'd ever come out again. Then the lure of sweetmeats had brought him up the spout before he was stable on his feet. Aminah had asked him to enter through the front gate so Idris and Barra could meet her uncle Omar. He'd used a cane to steady his steps.

Jinni emptied his glass as the thawb's falcons transformed

into monkeys swinging from tree to tree. "Amazing," he said. "This Ahab is a magician."

Aminah laughed. "Everyone in Damascus is sure of it, but not because of magic thawbs. It's his skill with needle and thread. Already the Sultan has him sewing for his entire court. May I pour you another sherbet, Uncle Omar?"

Jinni smiled greedily and nodded. "The world will soon be at his door. It is what you wanted?"

"Oh yes, it's perfect. And better yet is Khalidah."

"They are very happy," he said, taking the glass Aminah held out to him. "More so than most humans."

"You didn't cast a love spell, did you?" she asked. "You promised you wouldn't do it that way."

"I told you that I did not. Told you five times—this makes six. Why do you keep asking?"

"Aren't you the one who said, 'If you see a lion's teeth, do not take it for a smile?'"

He frowned. "For the last time, I found the ideal match. I arranged for them to meet and, with a little magic, I hastened the courtship. But I did not cast a love spell. You would know by now, Miss—"

"I'm Zubaydah, remember? Not Miss. Omar and his niece Zubaydah. You agreed to call me that in front of Idris and Barra, so you may as well get some practice."

"Yes, *Zubaydah*. As I was saying, you would know by now. Love spells are fleeting. It already would have faded."

"Yes," Aminah agreed. "You worked wonders, Uncle Omar. Forgive me for doubting you. More sweetmeats?"

"I *am* running a bit low," he said. "Yes, hand me that other tray."

Aminah set the delicacies in front of Jinni and poured him yet another sherbet.

"They are up to twenty children," she said, twirling about the room, the shimmering thawb billowing around her. Monkeys, growing long and thin, dropped from the branches. In an instant, king cobras, hoods spread and tongues flicking, swayed from side to side.

"I know," said Jinni.

"And in a new place, with room to grow. And the children—even the girls—are in school."

"And Khalidah loves them all. Yes, yes, I know! May we play chess now?"

Aminah sighed. "You always were the sentimental one in the family, Uncle Omar. By the way, Idris is suspicious of you. I think he's suspicious of everyone—even me."

"And why is that?" Jinni asked.

"Idris overheard me talking to you one night. When I wouldn't tell him who was in my quarters, he was furious. He's barely spoken to me since—not that I've seen much of him. The last time he surfaced, he wanted to know why I'd never mentioned you—my father's only brother. I told him that you'd been gone from Al-Kal'as for years—with no word—and that we all thought you were dead."

"A poor child finds herself with wealth and a long-lost uncle suddenly appears. Idris is wise to be suspicious. Perhaps I misjudged that boy. He may have a redeemable quality or two, after all."

"Well, I think he's surly and ungrateful."

"Yes. As I said, redeemable qualities."

Aminah rolled her eyes.

"Now, are you ready to lose another match?"

"Let me change first. I can't let Barra see this." The cobras had become elephants marching trunk to tail, and the thawb was glowing like wind-fed embers. "I made Ahab promise he'd never sell another like this. Or anything enchanted."

Jinni sniffed. "Demon magic. How terrible."

"For Ahab, it *would* be terrible," she said, disappearing into her sleeping chamber. "And you know it."

"Yes," said Jinni. "And doing good deeds is terrible for me."

"I'm still itching from the orb's rash, you know," Aminah called out. "I'm glad you're feeling better, Jinni. You need to be in good shape for the next wishing moon."

Jinni grunted. "Just like a human. No compassion."

She stepped from her room, dressed in a plain blouse and sarwal. "Let's take the board out into the garden."

Jinni nodded and began gathering the chess pieces.

Aminah touched his sleeve. "I'm so happy you're here with me," she said.

Uncle Omar's hand froze as he reached for the two kings, and a deep shade of fuchsia rose into his tanned cheeks.

"You're blushing," said Aminah. "I've embarrassed you."

He finished collecting the chessmen and tucked the board under his arm. "I am looking forward to playing under the stars," he said, gazing out the window and into the twilit garden. "Playing chess under the stars with my most excellent niece."

☽

AMINAH ROSE the next morning with the cry of the muezzin. Since finding Ahab, her nightmares had stopped altogether, and she awakened rested and refreshed—and even more determined to find someone else to help.

Idris hadn't mentioned spies lurking in the neighborhood since the night he'd come at her with a knife, and so fears that the Princess would find her lessened. She even felt secure enough to search within the city for her next project. Aminah was anxious to help her own people.

On the first evening of the new month, Aminah set the blue vase in front of her door, then rubbed Barra's salve all over her body and downed an ample portion of headache powder. "Preventative measures," she'd told Jinni the night before. Then, under the gleam of the wishing moon, Aminah brought out the orb.

She connected with it in an instant, the surge of raw energy bringing her to her knees. She closed her eyes against the brilliant red light, flashing like a beacon from the core of the magic crystal. The scene that followed showed Al-Kal'as as if from the eye of an eagle soaring far above it.

Aminah didn't direct the orb to show one thing or another. It happened automatically, as if the orb were her own mind. She and the crystal's spirit merged to scan the city, and only when the image locked on a bakery in the oldest section of Al-Kal'as did she realize that her eyes were still closed. She opened them to see in the orb what she'd been seeing in her head.

Too enthralled to be surprised, Aminah peered into the crystal, watching a group of shabby people gather in the dark street outside the bakery. Then she heard them speak.

"No bread left for himself, after he gives to everyone."

"A wonder he keeps his shop open. Nothing much to sell when he's feeding half of Al-Kal'as!"

"The fool! He'll soon be in the gutter with the rest of us. Still, may the blessings of Allah fall upon his honorable head."

As with Ahab, she sensed the power of a pure heart. Its gentle strength flowed through the walls of the bakery. "Here is another human untouched by greed, Jinni," she said, as the image in the orb changed to show the shop's interior.

A young man stood with his back to Aminah. She was surprised by his age. She'd expected such a grand heart to beat in the chest of someone older—someone whose wisdom and strength had come with the years.

The baker peered into several tall flour jars. He sighed and shook his head. Without seeing inside them, Aminah knew the jars were empty.

The young fellow swayed, as though he were light-headed. He reached out to steady himself as the image shifted, bringing the baker face-to-face with Aminah.

"Hassan!" she cried.

)

AMINAH WAS CONFUSED. There was no doubt this was the same Hassan who'd found her asleep in the desert. But she recalled that Hassan's father was a wealthy merchant who sent his personal caravans all over the Arab world. Hadn't he given his son responsibility for the caravan that had brought him to Al-Kal'as? Yet here he was shaking his head over empty flour jars in a run-down bakery.

He'd lied to her, she supposed. But would the orb have chosen a liar? It didn't seem possible.

Aminah's mind separated from the crystal, which went blank in an instant. She stood for a moment, until a bout of dizziness passed, and then carried the orb to its hiding place.

As she set it on the shelf, her eyes fell on Hassan's water skin, decorated with silver bands that were studded with sapphires. She realized now that the skin had been his most valuable possession, yet he'd insisted she keep it. He'd cared more for a beggar girl than for himself. Then she thought of his gaunt face and weak knees. He was going hungry while he handed out bread to half the city.

The orb was right about him, of course. Hassan was the one she should help. Even without the crystal, she knew his heart from firsthand experience. So if he'd lied to her, she was certain there had been a good reason.

Aminah spent the next morning nursing a slight headache and scratching at a new case of the rash, but her face didn't swell, just as the wizard had promised. And applying Barra's salve before using the orb had kept the worst of the itching at bay. She rubbed in more of the ointment, preparing for an afternoon walking the suq with Barra. It wouldn't do to be scratching and wriggling as if she were infested with fleas.

Though she no longer felt the need to buy very much, Aminah still enjoyed poking through the market's stalls. Or accompanying Idris into harness shops, laughing as he caressed a bridle or saddle like a lover.

She frowned at the thought of Idris. Aminah hadn't seen him for days, though it was clear he was nearby—the horses were well-groomed and fed. And sometimes she'd visit the stables only to find one of the stallions missing.

Between her worry about Idris and her puzzlement over Hassan, Aminah had trouble concentrating on their outing. She let Barra's comfortable chatter wash over her, seldom joining in.

"Oh, look there!" Barra cried, and the rise in her voice

pulled Aminah from her private thoughts. She followed Barra's pointing finger to see a troupe of performing monkeys dancing and leaping in the air to the music of their master's pipe. But it wasn't just the monkeys that had seized Barra's attention. Idris was an arm's length from the performance, watching with intense fascination.

Aminah moved to stand next to him. Idris glanced at her, then back at the monkeys. "I've always loved the funny little things," he said. "Like tiny people, don't you think?"

"Yes, I suppose so," Aminah answered. "But they can be nasty. One bit my finger when I was six, and I've been scared of the little brutes ever since."

"Look there," said Idris. "A monkey pyramid." At least a dozen of the furry creatures had climbed on one another to form a perfect triangle. Idris reached out as if to topple them.

Barra pushed forward to grab his sleeve and pull him away. "Keep your hands to yourself! Didn't you hear? They bite."

Aminah smiled. It's what her mother would have done—the mother she'd almost forgotten.

"Where have you been?" she asked Idris.

Without answering, he motioned for them to follow him through the crowd. When they reached the suq's fountain, Idris nodded in the direction of a storyteller, who was spinning the tale of Sindbad's seventh voyage. The storyteller noticed Idris and grinned.

"You seem to be friends," said Aminah.

"He's taught me many stories. Sometimes I tell a story in his stead."

"So that's what's been keeping you away from us," she said. They drew closer to hear better, but instead of listening,

Aminah stared at the look of pure rapture on Idris's face.

Barra noticed, too. "He's in love," she whispered in Aminah's ear, then chuckled at her shocked expression. "With story making."

Aminah was surprised at the hollow feeling in her stomach at the thought of being second best. Smiling at her silliness, she nudged Idris to get his attention, but she might as well have nudged a rock.

They'd arrived late in the story, so it wasn't long until the last word finally broke the spell. With a wave to the storyteller, who was about to start again, Aminah pulled Idris away from the fountain. "Come home, Idris," she said. "I miss you."

"I'm home almost every night," he said. "You just don't see me."

"You know what I mean. I want to have supper with you. I want to gaze at the stars, like we used to. We could play chess in the garden. Do you know the game?"

"No, but you have your dear uncle Omar for that," he said. "I suppose he's still hanging around."

"He comes and goes," she answered, irked by his sardonic tone. "Give him a chance, Idris. I think you could be friends—like we are."

"Friends." Idris sighed and gave her a sad smile. "I'm busy tonight, but I'll be there tomorrow evening for Barra's delicacies."

"Thank you," said Aminah.

"I must be off, now." He took a few steps, then turned back to her. "I'm still watching the house, Zubaydah. I haven't forsaken you."

He raised his hand in a brief salute and melted into the crowd.

☽

SEEING IDRIS unsettled Aminah rather than calmed her. In an effort to curb her lonely, restless feelings, she tried focusing on her mission to help Hassan. Impatient to take action, she urged Barra to start on supper the moment they got home.

When the meal—roasted chicken stuffed with rice—was ready, Aminah loaded two trays and said, "I'm tired. I think I'll eat in my suite tonight."

Barra gave her a concerned look. "Is anything wrong, dove?" she asked.

"No, I'm fine. I'll just have a little nibble and get some rest."

"A little nibble?" Barra stared at the chicken and the bowls piled high with dates, nuts, cucumbers, and fresh fruit. "You aren't expecting Omar, are you?" she asked hopefully.

"No." Aminah smiled. "You'd be the first to know if he was coming."

"Then why all the food?"

"I might get hungry in the night," said Aminah.

"All right, then," said Barra, who was growing accustomed to occasional odd behavior from her young mistress. "I'll help carry the platters to your room."

After the food was laid out in her quarters, Aminah kissed Barra's cheek. "Thank you."

Barra kissed her in return. "Let's have no monkey nightmares, you hear?"

They both laughed, and a moment later Aminah was alone. She waited for Barra to make her way back to the kitchen before setting the blue vase outside the door. Then she hurried to the lamp, summoning Jinni before the chicken could cool.

He spotted the feast and changed from purple demon to Uncle Omar in a wink.

"It's all for you," said Aminah. "I hope it's what you like."

He brandished a chicken leg in thanks, his mouth already too full to answer.

She left him and closed herself in her bedchamber—Jinni was too busy to notice she was gone. She dabbed ointment on the worst spots, donned her magical thawb, and checked the orb for a safe landing place. When Aminah returned to the outer room, Jinni was leaning back, sipping sherbet.

"I'm off to see our next Ahab," Aminah said, fixing her hijab in place.

"Your thawb is at it again," said Jinni.

She looked down. Nine planets were spinning around a blazing sun. Twinkling stars peppered the dark background.

"Galileo would approve," he said. "In fact, that thawb could teach him a thing or two."

"Who?" asked Aminah.

"Never mind."

"Please don't do that."

"Do what, Miss?"

"Say mysterious things and then not explain."

"I speak of the future," said Jinni, taking a handful of nuts. "Galileo will see far into the heavens with a telescope."

"With a tele—? Oh, never mind."

"That's what I said, Miss. Never mind."

Aminah glared at him. "I'm in a hurry. We'll talk about this . . . this Galileo later. Keep eating."

"If you insist," said Jinni, reaching for a bowl of nuts.

· Sixteen ·

AMINAH MOVED BACK into her bedchamber and stood with her eyes closed, envisioning a bare patch of floor near the bakery's entrance. As usual, stinging cold stabbed at her, and the hair on her arms stood on end. *Will I ever get used to this?* Aminah thought, as she was jerked from the room.

She'd forgotten to imagine both feet planted on the floor and materialized a hand's breadth above it. Her sandals smacked the stones as she landed, and Hassan, who was reaching deep inside a tall flour jar, jumped at the sound, whacking his skull on the rim. Rubbing his head, he turned to face her.

At that moment, the thawb decided to show off. Dozens of blazing comets streaked across the starry skies. They sizzled and shrieked as they looped around the planets and dove into the sun with stunning explosions. Hassan cried out and leapt behind his jars.

Aminah raised her arms, gaping at the wild display. It was the first time the thawb had produced sounds. "I never know what to expect," she said. "Don't worry, Hassan. It's harmless."

"But are you?" he asked, only his eyes visible above the jars. "Is your magic divine or satanic?"

"Oh, bother!" She took a step forward, and he scrambled backward, standing. "I'm not the devil. I'm here to help you."

Hassan studied her eyes. "Who are you? How do you know my name?"

"I'm magical, remember? Look, I am a very busy . . . a very busy . . . angel. If you want my help, stop wasting my time. I see you're out of flour."

"And salt," said Hassan. His sharp laughter was bitter. "My father was right; I ruin everything I touch."

"Did you ruin the people you've been feeding?"

He shrugged. "My kindness is killed by my lack of wisdom. The jars are empty, and I've no way to refill them. If only I'd been a better tradesman . . ."

"You didn't sell a single loaf, did you?" asked Aminah.

He shook his head. "There were too many starving mouths. I couldn't bake bread fast enough. I worked day and night, with no thought for tomorrow, and now I've nothing left to give. Not even to myself."

"I'm here to help," said Aminah.

"What can you do for me? Besides, the foolish don't deserve help."

"I can fill your jars."

"You'd do that?" His face brightened. "I'll run the bakery more like a business this time, I promise. Half to the poor, half to paying customers. In time, I'll repay you."

"No need for that. I'll return soon, Hassan." She pulled the thawb tightly about her and vanished.

Back in her bedroom, Aminah could hear the disgusting sounds of Jinni stuffing himself. She took the orb from its cradle and then crept forward, peering around the corner with dreadful fascination.

"There you are," he said, spotting her immediately. "Just a moment, please." He drained his gold cup, filled it, and drained it again.

"I'm glad you're enjoying yourself," said Aminah. "I'll roast a whole lamb for you next time, though I'm afraid you won't feel like eating for a week or two." She gestured toward the wishing moon, its round face framed by the window.

Jinni's grin faded, and he attacked the rest of the food with wolflike ferocity. Repulsed, Aminah looked on as he crammed his face with the remnants of the chicken. Next, he ate every date and every sweetmeat left on the platter. His head swelled to twice its size in order to accommodate everything, and then he dumped a bowl of olives into his cavernous mouth, eating pits and all. He smacked and dribbled on his chest as he chewed and swallowed, then grabbed the last pitcher of sherbet and drained it in seconds. During those few moments, he couldn't have looked less like Omar.

Aminah let him finish and then said, "Don't worry, I'm not making my wishes tonight."

"You might have told me sooner," Jinni grumbled, then belched with such force that Aminah covered her ears. "Ahh! Eating makes me feel almost human again."

"Almost human *again*? What do you mean?"

"What an odd thing for me to say." Jinni stroked his beard. "I wonder if . . . back when I had a name . . . No, impossible."

"I think you're remembering."

"Remembering what, Zubaydah?"

"Life before you became a jinni."

He shook his head. "I have always been a jinni."

"But—"

"I have *always* been a jinni," he said again.

"Fine. Have it your way."

"When it comes to my past life, I certainly will." He belched again and then smiled at her through food-encrusted teeth.

"I've created a monster," Aminah said.

"What you have created is a jinni with a satisfied stomach. Must we ruin such an agreeable evening with pointless conversation? Could we not play chess or backgammon instead? I know! It is still early. I will come for a visit as Uncle Omar, and we can have a torch-lit game of balls and mallets with that delightful young fellow—what is his name?"

"Idris."

"Yes, Idris and . . ."

"Barra."

"Yes, yes. Idris and Barra. What do you say? In fact, why not allow me to stay in one of your extra rooms tonight. No sense squeezing into the lamp with a full stomach. Would not be pleasant. Not pleasant at all."

Aminah sighed. "That wouldn't be wise, Jinni. And I don't have time for balls and mallets tonight. Besides, Idris isn't here."

His shoulders sagged, and before his expression could grow any more morose, she said, "But tomorrow night Idris will be here. You must come for dinner. And afterward, I'd like you to teach Idris chess."

"Ah," said Jinni, his eyes lighting. "A good plan."

Aminah reached into her pocket and brought out the orb. She felt the rash in her armpits prickle as thick crimson mists swirled, then parted, to show the bakery.

"I have something to show you," she said, scratching happily. "Meet Hassan."

)

HASSAN SAT ALONE, staring at the empty shop for what seemed an eternity and wondering if he'd imagined the girl in the shining robe. "I haven't eaten in three days," he said aloud to himself, "and now I'm starting to see things."

He turned back to the tall jar, trying to scrape together a handful of flour, but it was no use. He gave up and sat against the wall, thinking about the next day. He'd close the bakery, sell the equipment for a few coins, and join the beggars in the street. Then, as if to confirm his dim future, the flame from his only lamp sputtered and went out.

Sitting alone in the gloom, Hassan dozed off, but the moment his eyes closed, the room filled with a warm, red glow. He looked up and saw Aminah standing in front of him, her thawb gleaming like molten iron. Its brocaded surface showed rows of ovens spitting out loaves of bread. They fell downward, collecting in piles at the hem.

Aminah shielded her eyes, peering into the dark. "Where's your light?" she asked.

"No oil," he answered, not at all sure he wasn't dreaming.

The fiery glow winked out. Several minutes passed, then she was back, a brass lamp in each hand. Her robe dimmed, until the lamps alone lit the room.

Hassan rose and crept closer to her. "I thought you were a dream," he said. "Maybe you are."

Aminah thrust the lamps into his hands. "Do these feel like dreams?" she asked. "Careful, don't burn yourself."

Hassan stared at her, openmouthed. At first she didn't understand, then her hand flew to her face. She'd forgotten to replace the hijab.

"I know you," he said. "The beggar girl outside the gates of Al-Kal'as." He pointed to the scar on her forehead. "With a wound like that one. But how can this be?"

"It cannot. You're mistaken," she said.

"No, I'm not. It is you, Aminah. But don't be afraid. Your secret is safe."

"My secret? No, I have no secret, Hassan. I am not this Aminah. You are delirious with hunger. Here, I brought you some food." She pulled a bag from her shoulder.

Hassan smiled. "At first, I thought you might come to me for bread. After all, you were poor—or so I thought. Then in time you slipped from my memory—until now. Do you still possess the water skin?"

Aminah sighed. "Yes, Hassan."

"Were you an angel when I found you on the sand?"

"I lied," she said. "I'm not an angel. But you lied about being from a rich family, so we're even."

"I suppose I did stretch the truth," he said. "The caravan you saw was my father's—until we reached Al-Kal'as. Then all of it, down to the last camel, went to your Sultan to pay our debt."

"You don't need to explain," said Aminah.

"Want to hear something funny?" he asked. "Father always said I'd be the one to destroy his business, and I never doubted him. I was too generous, he said. Couldn't drive a hard bargain. Then Father died, and creditors descended on my mother and me like vultures. The business was already in ruins—had been for ages. My mother died a poor woman two months later."

"Nothing was left?"

"Nothing. It was better for me to leave Sidon—the city of my birth. Not everyone got his money, so I wasn't popular. I delivered the final caravan to Al-Kal'as and decided to stay. Buying the bakery took every copper carat I had. And as you see, Father was right about me."

"Yes," said Aminah. "You're a colossal failure—if you're counting dinars. But I'm counting saved lives, Hassan, and you're much better at that."

"You haven't tasted my bread," he said, setting the lamps on a shelf. "It's bad enough to take lives."

She laughed, dropping the bag into his hands. "Here, you need to eat."

"If you're not an angel, what are you?" he asked.

"Eat," she said.

Hassan crammed a handful of dates into his mouth.

"Slow down. You'll make yourself sick."

"Sorry," he said, when at last he could speak. "I must look like a starving jackal."

Aminah let him eat in silence, but when the dates and bread were gone, she said, "You weren't supposed to recognize me. It makes things . . . more difficult."

"Yes, that's so. I can't take your money now."

"What? That's ridiculous! I took your water skin with its silver and sapphires."

"It was my father's. I wanted to be rid of it."

"Remember the old saying? Please don't be grateful, for you will repay me. I never really thanked you for the skin, so now I'm repaying."

She reached into her money belt and unloaded a thousand

dinars, stacking them in front of him. "You probably thought the stones were glass. I could get twice this for them, so consider yourself cheated."

Hassan stared at the money. "You were a beggar girl," he said. "With a single gold ducat and a bad back."

"And you were once a wealthy merchant's son. Things change."

"But how?"

"I'm glad I found you, Hassan. But knowing about me is dangerous. You must tell no one. Promise?"

He nodded, his hot eyes boring into her.

Before she could stop herself, Aminah reached up to touch his cheek, and he put his hand over hers.

"I must go," she said, stepping away from him.

"But why—"

"No questions," she said. "There is more waiting for you than these dinars—much more. Watch for miracles, Hassan."

"Will I see you again? Do you still live in Al-Kal'as?"

Aminah smiled, put a finger to her lips, and disappeared.

)

AMINAH SPENT THE NEXT MORNING deciding how best to use her wishes for Hassan, but she found it difficult to concentrate. She'd be thinking of flour jars or ovens when the memory of Hassan's hand covering hers would send all other thoughts flying from her head. *It's silly, of course,* she said to herself, but she wasn't prepared for the unexpected and unexplainable rush of feelings that washed over her each time. In spite of this, she managed to come up with a satisfying plan for Hassan's bakery.

Idris arrived in the early evening, a storyteller's feathered turban on his head. He went to his room to change, and Aminah hurried to summon Uncle Omar. Thirty minutes later, she, Idris, and Barra met him at the gate.

Though Barra had treated Uncle Omar with respect before, on this visit she lavished him with care. If Jinni did have deeply hidden human roots, they seemed to surface with Barra's attention. Aminah found it amusing to watch them showering one another with compliments.

"Undoubtedly the finest touch with a rack of lamb in culinary history," said Uncle Omar as they settled on the rooftop terrace.

"You are too kind, sir," said Barra. It was too dark to tell, but Aminah wouldn't have been surprised to see Barra blushing.

Omar turned to Idris. "I hear I am to instruct you in the fine art of chess, my boy."

Idris looked up in surprise.

"I forgot to tell you," said Aminah.

"I sense a sharp mind," Omar continued. "It will not be long until I will be losing to you."

Aminah was amazed. Was this her Jinni speaking? Impostor or not, his words were having the proper effect. Idris smiled.

"Shall we descend to the garden and begin?" Omar asked, and Idris nodded. "Then later, perhaps, you can regale us with a tale or two. I hear you are a storyteller without peer."

"I *am* quite good," said Idris, still smiling.

"Excellent! We will gather back on the terrace when the lesson is done."

"It'll be a treat for all of us," said Aminah. "We don't hear much from Idris these days."

Idris turned a cool eye on her. She was alarmed at first, but then he grinned and her moment of wariness passed.

Uncle Omar sighed. "Unfortunately, the lesson must be a short one, and I have time for but one brief tale." He looked at Barra and shrugged. "I have not yet secured a room at the kahn, so I must not be too late."

Barra melted under his gaze and said, "Oh no, there'll be no kahn for you, especially at this time of night. Shame on you, Miss Zubaydah, for not inviting your uncle to stay."

Aminah hadn't seen this coming, though later she realized Jinni's highly polished manners should have been a clue. All she could do was agree that she'd been thoughtless and ask Barra to prepare a room for dear Uncle Omar. Jinni flashed her a broad smile, and she couldn't help smiling in return.

Jinni was right about Idris. He picked up the game with astonishing speed. Aminah was pleased the lesson didn't drag on, and that Idris told only one story—the rather brief tale of "The Blind Man, Baba Abdullah." She wanted to get Jinni alone and make her wishes for Hassan.

As Idris finished the story, and everyone—especially Uncle Omar—doused him with praise, Aminah yawned. Much to her delight, it proved contagious, and soon the rest of them couldn't keep their jaws together. In a matter of minutes, everyone agreed to call it a night.

Wasting no time, Aminah bolted her door and rubbed the lamp. Jinni wasn't inside, of course, but she hoped a good rubbing would still summon him—and it did. Since his apartment was next to hers, he simply walked through the wall.

"Not tonight, Miss," he said, his chin drooping. "I am fatigued beyond words. No wishes, please."

Aminah laughed. "Jinn grow tired? Good try, Uncle Omar. By the way, mark one for you. Barra played into your hands perfectly. And though I could still send you back to the lamp, I won't—if you'll do your best with my wishes."

"Do not ruin the best evening in memory," Jinni begged. "Please."

"I'm sure the effects won't be so bad this time. Why, using the orb hardly bothers me at all anymore, so I'm certain it will be the same for you."

"But what happens if I am near death for three or four days? You don't know how to take care of sick demons. And what would Barra say? And Idris?"

Jinni looked so miserable, Aminah almost agreed to give him another day of reprieve. "If that happens, then I'll send you back to the lamp. I'll tell Barra you had an early business appointment. And I swear I'll bring you back as soon as you feel better."

"You swear?"

"On my father's grave."

"Perhaps I will feel better, not being cooped up," said Jinni. "Fresh air and room to move about might make all the difference."

"Do we have a deal? Your best with my wishes for some decent time outside the lamp?"

Jinni nodded.

· Seventeen ·

WITH HIS STOMACH FULL but his mind reeling, Hassan fell into a fitful sleep soon after Aminah left him. Nightmares of the starving women who scratched at his bakery door—and the children with bloated bellies—woke him. Lying in the dark, he worried again that Aminah had been a dream. He rose and stumbled to the table. His fingers searched, finding the pile of dinars, and he sank to his knees in relief. It was all true!

Exhausted to the core by continuous worry and hunger, Hassan slipped back into his bed, feeling at peace for the first time in weeks. In his head, he counted and recounted the coins, planning for daylight. He'd go to the suq and buy flour, salt, and fuel for the ovens. He'd pick up sugar, spices, and more. But first he'd make a sign for the door: BREAD THIS AFTERNOON.

Planning to make a sign was the last thing Hassan remembered, until telltale scratching at the back door awakened him. He yawned, followed by a long, bone-cracking stretch, and then smiled at the pleasant dreams he couldn't quite remember. The scratching turned to rapping, along with a chorus of whimpers. Suddenly Hassan was wide-awake. He leapt up, throwing open the shutters on his only window. The sun was high overhead and beginning its western slide.

He threw on a robe, wondering how he could have slept past midday, and ran his fingers through his hair. "You'll have bread within the hour," he called through the back door. Stuffing his pockets with dinars, he ran out the front.

In less than an hour, Hassan returned, pushing a cart filled with hard, round loaves. Three boys trailed behind, lugging bulging sacks.

Distributing bread to the desperate crowd behind his shop was a difficult, even dangerous, task. He couldn't simply set the bread out for the taking without starting a riot, and so he made them form an orderly line. By the time he'd placed a loaf in each grasping hand, the day was at an end.

Hassan had managed to save a loaf for himself. As darkness shrouded his shop, he lit one of Aminah's lamps and curled up on his tattered diwan to eat. He awoke later with bread still in his fist, amazed that he could be so tired after sleeping long into the day.

The lamp guttered, threatening to extinguish itself, and he rose to fetch the other. As he reached for the second lamp, his hand brushed a jar that hadn't been there before. It fell from the shelf, and Hassan held his breath as it dropped, waiting for it to shatter. Instead, it bounced twice and then rolled lazily in circles.

The jar was fiery red and looked like pottery, but the surface seemed smoother and cooler to his touch. It certainly wasn't one of his, which would have broken into a thousand pieces.

"I don't know where you came from," he said, "but I'll fill you with salt."

Hassan cried out in fear, flinging the jar away. Salt scattered across the floor as it flew through the air and crashed into the wall. Undamaged, it lay in the corner. He crept close, righting the vessel and peering inside. Salt still covered the bottom.

"Fill with salt," he said, his voice trembling. His eyes weren't fast enough to see it happening, but the jar was once again filled to the top.

He glanced nervously about the room and suddenly noticed the other jars in a variety of sizes and shapes, but all fiery red. His old containers were gone, and these stood in their place.

Hassan lifted another of the smaller jars—one he could afford to lose—and raised it above his head. By now, he was certain what would happen—or wouldn't happen—but still he shut his eyes and, grimacing, dropped it to the stones beneath his feet.

The jar skipped across the floor but remained in one piece. Hassan retrieved it. There wasn't so much as a chip on its fiery surface. Feeling bolder, he flung the jar at the wall with all his strength. It rebounded, narrowly missing his face, and landed without a mark.

Scratching his head in awe, Hassan moved to the largest jar, which was almost his own height. Peeking over its rim, he said, "Fill with flour. And make it wheat flour . . . please."

It was instantly filled to heaping.

"A miracle," whispered Hassan, who had been settling for barley flour until now.

He chose another vessel and filled it with olive oil. Another with sugar. Others with raisins and dates for making pastries. Smaller containers with spices.

Then Hassan tried filling one with gold coins, but nothing happened. He couldn't get rubies or emeralds, either. "Edibles only," he said, with a laugh, and decided to start a batch of bread.

As he mixed the dough, he thought to check the ovens.

Hoping they were still hot, he took the lamp and hurried outside, but the bricks barely warmed his fingertips. He cursed himself for forgetting the fires, even though there'd been no need for heated ovens an hour ago. He threw open the charcoal bin. It was empty, and his store of wood was gone, too.

Hassan rested his palm against the bricks and moaned. "I need you hot," he said, speaking to the oven as if it were an old friend.

He jerked his hand away, wincing with pain, and fanned it wildly in the cool, evening air. In an instant, the oven had become blistering hot. When Hassan recovered from the pain and shock, he peered into the firebox to find only ashes lying on the stones.

"I want you cold," he said, reaching out a tentative hand to touch the bricks. The oven was cold.

"Hot," he commanded. His cheeks burned and his brow beaded with sweat, and he stepped away from the intense heat.

Hassan ordered the ovens to cool and returned to his bread. He commanded one of the smaller vessels to fill with cold water, and then, instead of mixing the dough, he sat in a daze, soaking his stinging hand. *Jars that fill on request,* he thought. *And ovens that heat without fuel. What next?*

Milk! The idea exploded in his brain like a heavenly vision. Why not add milk to the bread dough? Or better yet, cream. He knew, as if he had always known, that the dough would be easier to handle and the bread would taste better. It wouldn't keep long, but bread went stale quickly, anyway—so quickly that people bought it daily, sometimes twice a day.

The results of Aminah's third wish flooded Hassan's mind

with unbelievable notions about baking. He thought of a better way to leaven his bread by using the yeast left over from wine making. He envisioned improved designs for ovens and concocted plans for amazing new pastries. His mind swelled with ideas until there was hardly room for another thought.

"Aminah's miracles," he said, then wished a jar full of cream.

)

"UNCLE OMAR CERTAINLY LOVES to eat," Idris whispered.

Barra nodded. They were wandering through the suq, trailing behind Aminah and Jinni. Omar would point to this delicacy and that, and Aminah would buy them for him. She'd just purchased a large cluster of grapes.

"He's like a little boy turned loose in a shop full of sweetmeats," said Idris.

Barra smiled. "I think it's adorable."

He snorted. "I think it's begging. Why can't he buy his own fruit?"

"Maybe you shouldn't have come," said Barra. "You seem so irritable."

"I do have other places to be," he said, "but I'm here now, so I'll stay."

Aminah looked back at Idris. "I don't think he trusts you yet," she whispered to Jinni. "Even after your flattery."

"As I told you, a smart boy. I sense he's wary of you, too," he said, popping a grape into his mouth. "Oh my! If I have ever tasted one of these, I cannot remember. Magnificent!"

It had taken the demon only five days to recover after granting the wishes for Hassan. It might have taken longer, but Barra proved not only willing but also eager to be his nurse.

(She hoped it wasn't her rack of lamb that had made him ill.)

Now, with a week gone by, Uncle Omar was walking the suq without leaning on his cane. But even though Jinni seemed in perfect shape, Aminah hadn't been able to get him back into the lamp. Of course, she could have forced him to return, but each time she suggested it, his unhappy face discouraged her from giving the command.

"There was a time I believed Idris would offer up his life for me, you know. Then things between us got . . . complicated," said Aminah.

"Love is a messy business," said Jinni.

"Who said anything about love?" she demanded. "Oh, I can't keep anything from you."

"Not true, but I am glad you think so."

Aminah laughed, then grew serious. "Maybe I should tell Idris about the lamp."

"Not wise," Jinni mumbled, around a mouthful of fruit. "He may seem trustworthy, but the lamp is too great a temptation. Heed my words. To possess it, I have seen sons turn against fathers. Daughters against mothers. And brothers against sisters."

"All humans aren't like that," she said. "Take Ahab, for instance. And Hassan . . ." She stopped, the sudden memory of Hassan's touch causing her heart to flutter. It wasn't so with Idris's touch—even his kisses. And yet she cared for both of them.

Jinni noticed the color rise in her cheeks when she said Hassan's name. His eyes narrowed, but in a congratulatory voice he said, "And include yourself on the list."

"Why, thank you, Jinni."

"However, you three are rare exceptions, though perhaps I would include Barra. An angel of mercy!"

"But I think Idris has real possibilities, too, and the only way to find out depends on you."

"That is absurd."

"You are a permanent part of my life now, Uncle Omar."

"Unless the Princess finds you."

"Thank you, Uncle," she said, frowning. "I needed reminding."

"I apologize," said Jinni, and Aminah sensed he was genuinely dismayed. "Once a jinni, always a jinni, I suppose. Sarcasm is in our nature."

"No, I was quite serious," said Aminah. "Sometimes I let myself forget the danger."

"You were saying I was a permanent part of your life . . ."

"Yes. And that means Idris must trust you—and like you—before he'll lower his guard."

"I see," said Jinni. "I will do all that is possible to win his favor."

"Truly?"

Jinni nodded.

"Good," she said, and called over her shoulder. "Idris, Uncle Omar would like to visit your favorite harness dealer. Barra and I will meet you back here in an hour."

Uncle Omar and Idris both seemed stunned but threw each other polite smiles and started off together.

Aminah watched them go, hoping she hadn't made yet another mistake, but then the sensation of Hassan's touch washed over her again. Thoughts of Idris and Jinni evaporated. The strange feeling excited Aminah, but because it frightened her, too, she hadn't visited the bakery again.

Barra placed her hand on Aminah's forehead. "You're flushed, child. Is something bothering you?"

"No, no, I'm fine," she said.

"You are redder yet," said Barra. "Come, let's have the truth."

Truth about what? Aminah wondered uneasily. *Can she have guessed about Jinni?*

"Is it Idris?" she asked with a sly smile. "I see how you look at him."

Aminah was so relieved that her laugh sounded forced. "Don't be silly. If I look at him in any way, it's with pity. He's either angry or absent these days."

Barra studied Aminah's face and raised an eyebrow.

"Really, I'm fine. Unless I have a fever."

"Flushed but no fever," said Barra. "Still, I think we should stay out of the sun as much as possible. So then, what shall we do for an hour?"

"I hear Perfumes of Eden has new scents from Damascus," said Aminah. "The way there is shady, and so I'd like to take a look."

Barra laughed. "More like try them all, I would have once said. But you've changed, Zubaydah."

They moved down the narrow streets, following a winding path around corners and through alleys, stepping around hempen bags full of spices or stopping to examine a new foreign delicacy at a grocer's stall. Aminah had never approached the perfumery from this direction, and suddenly she realized where she was. She and Barra had passed into an older section of Al-Kal'as with shabby buildings in need of repair. It was in this district that Hassan had his shop. In fact, it lay just ahead.

Aminah stopped, thrilled yet disquieted. "I'm not certain this is the right direction," she said. "I think we should go that way."

"No, Zubaydah. We pass into a better district after two more corners, then come upon the perfumery." Barra turned a questioning eye on her. "You know this better than I."

Without answering, Aminah started forward, realizing she wouldn't be able to pass the bakery without going in. *It's foolish*, she thought, *but I want to see him.*

As they drew near the shop's door, Aminah reached out to take Barra's arm. "Wait, we need bread."

"But we have bread delivered."

"I want to try a different baker, and I like the looks of this place."

Barra gaped at the worn storefront but said nothing. She followed Aminah through the narrow door. No one was inside. Aminah knew that "respectable" customers came to the front, so Hassan might be at the rear, distributing bread to the poor.

They waited a few silent moments, and then Aminah lost her nerve. She turned to go, but Hassan's voice stopped her.

"Pardon me. I'm sorry I wasn't here to greet you, Madam."

Aminah turned back, and Hassan's eyes widened. She lifted a finger to her lips. Barra was almost out the door and hadn't noticed.

"My good man," said Aminah. "I'll take two of your finest loaves."

"Ah," said Hassan, hiding a smile. "I have something new—

better than anything you've tasted." He pulled out a rounded loaf. "It's light as a feather and as tasty as fresh cream. Made from the finest wheat flour."

Aminah stared. "How did you get it to rise like this?"

"Yes, how?" asked Barra, drawing near.

"Here, sample it," he said, breaking off the end of the loaf.

"It's magic," said Aminah, handing the rest to Barra.

"Yes," said Hassan. "The bread of angels."

"Barra, go on to the perfumery. I'll find out what other marvels come from the ovens of . . . What is your name, sir?"

"Hassan."

"Come from the ovens of Hassan's bakery. I'll be along in a few minutes."

"I'll stay with you," Barra replied. "I wish to know his secrets as well. After all, I cook the meals." Her mouth settled into a stubborn line.

Aminah tried to think of a way to get rid of Barra, who stood with a suspicious smile beginning to crinkle the corners of her eyes. "Oh, let me do this alone," she said at last. "I need the practice if I'm ever to run a household on my own."

"I'm not much for perfume," said Barra, "but I'll get out of your way. Don't be long, Miss. I'll worry."

"Thank you, Barra!" Aminah knew she sounded much too grateful and, likely, much too eager.

With Barra out the door, Hassan moved forward and took Aminah's hand. "You've come back to me," he said, gazing into her eyes.

His real touch was much better than the memories. Before she could stop herself, Aminah reached for his other hand. "I shouldn't have come," she said. "It's too risky."

Gently pulling her forward, Hassan guided Aminah toward the magic jars. "They're amazing," he said. "Did you know that cream won't spoil when it's in one of them? I think that means oil won't go rancid, either, and wheat won't get the weevil. How did you do this, Aminah?"

"Don't call me that," she whispered.

"But it's your name."

"I am Zubaydah now. And don't speak of the jars or the ovens, even to me. If the wrong people find out about them, I'll be in terrible trouble. And so will you."

Hassan stared at her, then nodded. "Not a word, I promise. Thank you, Zubaydah. You saved my life."

Aminah smiled. "How did your beggars like this bread?"

"My experiment? They're wild about it. Trouble is it takes so much longer to make that I can't do it alone. I still bake a lot of flat bread because it's faster—lots of mouths to feed. Maybe I can solve the problem by putting a few beggars to work."

"Just don't let them see you filling jars or heating the ovens. But I agree, you need help. You've got to start selling to regular customers, or people will know something odd is going on. You can't run a bakery if you aren't making money, remember. So, I'll start you off by buying . . ."

"I'll deliver to your house. All you want. No charge, of course."

"No, I'll come here—or send Barra—and I'll pay. Either that, or I won't come back," she lied.

"Then pay, because I want to see you," Hassan said, holding her hands more tightly. "I want to sit and talk. Let me come to you."

She shook her head.

"Please."

Aminah pulled away. "I'll take two . . . no, make it four of your experiments," she said, sounding like nothing more than a customer. "And I hope you'll be doing pastries soon."

Hassan's face fell, and he turned to reach for the bread.

Aminah leaned forward, dropping several coins into his hand. "I'll come to you," she whispered. "Tonight."

· Eighteen ·

"**THE MAN KNOWS HORSES!**" Idris clapped Omar on the shoulder. "We're going for a ride—if you don't mind, that is."

Aminah hadn't seen Idris happier in weeks. Then she searched Jinni's eyes, wondering again if jinn rode horses. Or if the Powers allowed jinn that sort of freedom. What she found was an excitement as genuine as he showed for food. "I suppose it's been a while since you've been on a horse, Uncle Omar—as busy as you've been," she said.

He grinned. "Longer than I'd have liked."

"Have fun," she said, and watched in fascination as Jinni all but ran to the stables, he and Idris chattering like two school-boys off on an adventure.

When they returned, Aminah reminded Omar that he needed his rest. He disappeared into his room, only to reappear in her quarters a moment later.

"How was it?" she asked.

"Quite refreshing," he answered, but his look was unsettled.

"What's wrong, Jinni?"

"Memories. Of a past I never had. As I rode, I imagined once owning horses." He laughed. "Impossible!"

"Perhaps it was your former life," she said.

Jinni began to fidget. "I believe I need the rest you suggested. Well, then, off to my room. Good night."

"And *I* believe you're close to remembering," said Aminah. "Try harder."

"So tired," said Jinni, yawning. "A little food and a little sleep, that is what I need."

"I'm not stupid. I know jinn don't sleep. I think you're scared. You're running away from your past."

The fidgeting rose into Jinni's face, a nervous twitch settling in his right eye. If he had a response, he was too flustered to get it out. Instead, he turned into a light purple mist and vanished into the lamp.

Aminah stared after him, and it took her a moment to realize he'd returned to the lamp on his own. She decided he was running away in the only way possible for a jinni. She also decided to leave him there, at least until the next day. Aminah didn't have time for a confused demon, even one that occasionally reminded her of her father. She had an important visit to make.

She set the blue vase outside the door and changed into one of Ahab's plainer thawbs. She left her head uncovered—long, dark tresses cascading to her waist—and her face unveiled. While chewing mint leaves to freshen her breath, she dabbed on a little of the new scent she and Barra had purchased at Perfumes of Eden. Then, without checking the orb, she imagined herself in Hassan's shop.

He stood in the shadows, waiting, and when Aminah's feet touched the floor, he stepped into the light of lamps newly filled with oil. Without a word, he took her in his arms. They embraced in silence, his arms and chest forming a cocoon that filled Aminah with such warmth, such elation, that she wished they could stand there forever. But at last Hassan released her and stepped away.

"This was the only way I knew to tell you what I feel," he said.

"Is this happening too quickly?" Aminah asked. "Not that I mind, really."

Hassan's look was troubled. "It's a fair question to ask. Perhaps I'm hurrying this along in order to secure your magic for myself. How could you know otherwise?"

"Are you?"

"No, of course not."

"There is another way to look at this," said Aminah. "Perhaps you should be afraid of my powers. If you make me angry, perhaps I could be dangerous."

"My heart tells me otherwise."

"And so does mine," she said. "Could we start over again—with no words, I mean?"

Hassan smiled, and pulling her close, he kissed her. It was a delicate kiss, but it brushed her lips with fire.

☽

HASSAN KEPT A SPOT near the door free of buckets, jars, and baskets. That way Aminah could make her nightly visits without consulting the orb. He soon learned that the subtle aroma of jasmine-scented perfume announced her arrival, and he would be there either to embrace her or—with childlike exuberance—to stuff his newest pastry creation into her mouth.

For Aminah, the bakery became an oasis. She hadn't realized the strain of being someone else, and so when they were alone, she consented to Hassan's using her real name. Behind barred doors and shuttered windows, she could be herself with him—or close to it, at least. As pleasant and reassuring as it was to be with Barra—and, at times, with Idris and Jinni—it was nothing like being with Hassan.

She told him about her father and mother, about her days on the streets as a beggar. He grew somber when her words painted a grim picture of Beggars' Corridor. He laughed when she described bathing naked in the sea. She recounted the amazing story of Talib and Hasim—or at least as much as she could without revealing the lamp. It would have jeopardized both of them if she had; and for the same reason, she did not tell him where she lived. He accepted both her secrecy and her magic; and for a time, he didn't ask more about either one.

Hassan had little more of his story to tell, though Aminah coaxed from him memories of a happy childhood—"the days before Father became so critical of me," he told her. Aminah seemed to have more to say, and he was content to listen. Often he'd take her hand as she spoke, and his touch became as natural as her own breathing.

During the day, Aminah tried to act as though nothing unusual was going on in her life, but Barra seemed to see right through her.

"Spare a thought for your work. You'll cut off a finger," Barra said one afternoon, while Aminah was helping her chop vegetables for supper. "It's that young baker, isn't it? I knew the moment I saw you together, though it's a mystery how you manage to spend time with him."

Aminah stared at her, not knowing how to answer.

"I'd hoped you and Idris—" Barra smiled. "Listen to me. You'd think I was your mother."

"You *are* my mother, Barra," said Aminah.

Tears filled Barra's eyes. She encircled Aminah with her arms and kissed her cheek. "How could I have misread the looks that passed between the two of you?" she asked, shaking her head.

"I do love Idris—but not in that way."

"And the baker?"

Aminah sighed. "His name is Hassan, and I am in love with him. We met in the desert months ago—before you came into my life. Even before Idris. I mustn't tell you anything more—not now, at least—so please don't ask."

"As you wish. You'll tell me when the time is right," said Barra, whose eyes suddenly widened. "Oh, Idris, there you are. Have you been with the horses?"

Aminah turned to find Idris standing rigid in the doorway. The look on his face was frightening, and she knew he'd been there long enough to hear about Hassan. He stumbled backward and then rushed from the kitchen.

"Go," said Barra, and Aminah hurried after him.

"Idris!" she called. "Stop! Please, stop!"

He paused at the gateposts, not turning to look at her.

"I'm sorry you had to hear it that way," she said.

"It's like everything else with you," he said bitterly. "At least Barra warrants some trust from the secretive Zubaydah—or whoever you are."

"Give me a little more time, Idris. Then you'll know everything."

"I know enough, I guess. Have a happy life with your baker. I won't be around for the wedding, so I'll congratulate you now."

"Don't leave. I love you like a brother, Idris. You're my family." Her voice broke.

He still hadn't turned to look at her, and she reached for his arm to pull him around. He shook her hand away. "I can't do this. Don't you see? It's precisely because you love me like a brother that I can't stay."

She watched him go, hot tears cooling on her cheeks. He never looked back.

❭

"GIVE HIM TIME," said Hassan. "He'll think this through and realize you mean too much to him." He dabbed the corners of Aminah's eyes with the hem of his jubba.

"Do you really believe that?" Aminah asked.

"Yes . . . no. I suppose I really don't know. I just want you to be happy."

She cradled his head in her hands, kissing him on each cheek and then on the lips. The last kiss was both tender and eager. "Thank you," she said.

Hassan grinned. "You're most welcome. Now, as much as I hate to cut the rewards of your gratitude short, the hour grows late and the baking must begin."

"I'll stay and help you," Aminah said. "I don't want to be alone."

Hassan stroked her cheek. "I'd like that, but you needn't work. Just sit and talk to me."

She kissed him again and then pushed away. "You think I'll be more trouble than help, I suppose. Well, I'll show you."

Hassan smiled, pulling her close to him again. "I figure you can work circles around me. I was just being polite."

"Polite? So you didn't really mean it, then. You want all the work out of me you can get. Is that it?" The teasing eased her misery. Aminah raised her chin in mock anger.

"What have I done," he said, laughing and shaking his

head. "What have I done, getting caught up with the likes of you?"

As he gazed into her eyes, Hassan suddenly sobered. "Where is this leading us, Aminah?"

"To a life together," she answered.

"Only after dark? Always cloaked in mystery? I want the light of day to shine on us, Aminah. I need to be trusted with your secrets."

She dropped her head onto his shoulder, saying nothing. She realized he was right. This was playing at romance. She had been ignoring the hard questions. Like Idris, Hassan couldn't be expected to wait much longer for full entry into her life.

"Aminah?" he asked, breaking the long silence.

"I love you, Hassan." It was the first time she had told him so directly, and his body trembled at her words. "That's part of the reason I have kept secrets from you. Please believe me."

"But it can't be this way," he said.

"Then I will tell you everything. Not tonight, but soon. I still need a little time."

Hassan sighed.

"We'll be together—in the sunlight," she promised. "But I can tell you this much: it cannot be in Al-Kal'as."

"As if staying here is important," he said. "I'll go anywhere, Aminah. Name the spot, and we are gone."

She nodded. "Give me until the moon is full. That's all I ask. You should look for a buyer. It would be better to sell this place than abandon it."

With a shout of joy, Hassan bounded over to the flour jar,

dipping out a handful and tossing it at Aminah. Before she could recover, he grabbed her up and swung her around.

"Put me down," she squealed, laughing. "We have work to do."

$$)$$

EVEN THOUGH Idris hadn't been much of a companion during the last month, his departure left Aminah feeling lonely again—when she wasn't with Hassan. As a remedy, she brought Uncle Omar out of the lamp to keep her company, careful to avoid any mention of his former life as a human.

As it turned out, he spent most of his time entertaining Barra. She prepared any dish he fancied, laughed at his jokes (though jinni humor was rarely funny), and batted her eyelashes at him from time to time, which Aminah found quite amusing. She also begged him to teach her chess, which Aminah found even more amusing.

One night, when Uncle Omar was to stay over, Aminah left him at the chessboard with Barra and excused herself. Out of habit, she set the blue vase outside the door before she made the leap to the bakery.

"Why does she do that?" asked Jinni, pointing to the vase.

"It's a sign that she isn't to be disturbed," said Barra. "So I suppose that means we'll be alone."

"Madam!" Jinni grinned and winked at her. "Pay attention to the game. It is your turn."

Barra laughed, then focused on the chessboard.

"Do you think my niece has been acting strangely?" asked Jinni, after waiting several minutes for Barra to make her move. "She moped a bit when Idris left—I do miss that boy— but now she seems too happy. Even giddy at times."

"You've ruined my concentration," said Barra, smiling. "Ah, well, now I have an excuse for losing. As for Zubaydah, she's in love."

Jinni's scowl erased her smile. "The baker!" he cried.

She cringed at the anger in his voice, and at the thought that she had betrayed Zubaydah's confidence. *How does he know about Hassan?* she wondered.

"I'm only guessing," said Barra. "It's just a silly old woman's speculation."

"You are not mistaken," he said, eyes flashing. "Forgive me, Madam. I am not feeling well. I must retire for the evening."

"I'm sorry to have upset you," she said. "Please don't go."

Her lip trembled, and Jinni, suddenly the kind Uncle Omar Barra recognized, took her hand. "You have no need to apologize, Madam. I am the silly one, not you. Please, do not tell my niece that I acted the fool. I have come to my senses. I am only her uncle, after all. She will tell me of this love when she is ready. Now, let us finish our game."

☽

THE NEXT WISHING MOON was a week away, and Aminah knew what she was going to do with her wishes—or at least one of them. During the following days, she studied her books with fierce intensity, searching for the ideal place to take Hassan—Barra, too, if she'd agree to come. And Idris, if he came back as Hassan suggested he would.

It would be difficult to leave the city of her birth—to leave behind the graves of her parents. She had hoped to make life better for the beggars of Al-Kal'as, but she could do that from anywhere. She'd get another house—overlooking the sea, she imagined—and begin a new life away from the Full Moon of

Full Moons. Then she and Jinni could continue as before. It was this realization that finally made the decision to leave possible.

After all her searching, Aminah wasn't surprised when she came back to the first spot that had leapt into her mind. Tyre was the perfect choice. They'd build a new home on the same hill above where she'd waded in the sea. What could be better?

Aminah could hardly wait to tell Hassan. It seemed as if the sun would never set that day. When at last darkness fell, she secured the lamp beneath her robe. Aminah had been leaving the lamp behind on her visits to the bakery, but now she hated to be separated from it. Nothing must go wrong during their last week in Al-Kal'as.

She made the leap and arrived to find an empty shop, doors and windows shut against the night. It was strange not to have Hassan standing right there, waiting for her. Still, Aminah knew he was somewhere close. She was about to call for him when angry voices from the back room froze her heart.

"What do I need with bread!" cried an oily voice. "I need dinars! Something strange is going on here, Hassan. At home, you didn't know an oven from a donkey's rump. Now you bake bread but never buy flour."

There was no answer, and soon the same man spoke again. "Yes, I've been watching you, old friend, and I know you have something to hide. But two hundred dinars will seal my lips. Four hundred erases my memory."

"And what happens when the dinars are gambled away, Rashid?" said Hassan's voice.

Aminah cocked her head at the name. Then she remembered Hassan's traveling companion, the one who'd accused her of stealing the gold ducat. Was this the same Rashid?

A short, stout man flew into the room, as if he'd been shoved. She recognized him right away. He still wore the same blue and yellow jubba, dirty and tattered now.

His eyes narrowed as he stared at Aminah's unveiled face, his eyes wandering to the scar on her forehead. She shivered, but he didn't seem to recognize her. Behind him, Hassan searched for something to say.

"My . . . cousin," he said. "Zubaydah."

"Cousins in Al-Kal'as?"

"Yes. Twice removed. I had forgotten they were here."

"Tell me, Zubaydah, how did you get in? The door is barred." Rashid licked his lips. "Make that five hundred, Hassan. I'll be back tomorrow night."

When Hassan didn't answer, Rashid unbarred the door. "Tomorrow," he said, then stepped into the dark.

Aminah pulled the door closed, securing it again. "You told him my name," she said.

Hassan fell against the wall, looking miserable. "I have a hundred cousins. I couldn't think of one. At least I didn't give him your real name."

"What will you do?" she asked.

"About Rashid?" He laughed. "What can he prove? Besides, I'm not violating the law. If you're worried, I'll make it look good by purchasing some flour."

"How did he find you?"

Hassan shrugged. "I haven't seen him since the day we found you lying in the sand. I assumed he returned home to Sidon."

A chill settled over her. Was it possible someone had led Rashid to the bakery? Idris, perhaps? She immediately hated herself for entertaining such a thought.

"Pay him," Aminah said.

"You're joking?"

"Pay him three times what he asks, on the condition he leaves Al-Kal'as with the next caravan. I'll give you the money."

"No! I won't give your money to the likes of Rashid."

"You must! Just this once." Aminah disappeared and was back in moments with a large leather purse. "Please, Hassan. We need this week to be without problems, and then we'll be gone."

"Why? Let's leave tonight."

"Don't make me explain. I've so much to tell you, but I can't think straight. Pay him!" Aminah pushed the money into Hassan's hands.

The tone of her voice silenced him, but he leaned in to kiss her. Hassan dropped the purse and folded Aminah into his arms, then took her slowly downward to his diwan. They sat in one another's tight embrace long into the night.

)

RASHID PATTED the money belt that now held fifteen hundred dinars. He was ready—even anxious—to leave Al-Kal'as, but it would be a week before the next caravan going his way departed. However, the delay had a bright side. It gave him time to visit the Sultan's palace.

Rashid expected the guards to turn him away at the gate, so he planned with care what he would say. When they gripped their scimitars and ordered him to leave, he leaned as near as he dared and whispered, "I have seen the lamp." In moments, he stood before the Sultan's daughter.

He bowed, kissing his fingertips and raising them to his brow. It was the homage reserved for her father, but Badr al-Budur didn't stop him. Her smile was thin as she asked, "What makes you believe I search for a lamp?"

"Rumors abound, oh effulgent one."

"There are many lamps in Al-Kal'as."

Rashid bowed again. "But there is magic in the one you seek."

Badr took a sharp breath and dismissed the guards, except for a tall man that stood by her side. When they were alone with Rashid, the Princess pulled a dagger from her belt and held it to his throat. Rashid didn't flinch—until she spoke again. Her voice was so low he strained to hear it, yet it cut through him like a razor.

"And what do you know of magic?" she whispered.

"Very little, Princess. I have only ventured to guess."

The tip of the dagger pricked his skin. A drop of blood swelled like an engorged tick, then broke and coursed down his neck.

"You waste my time with guesses? Saladin, this worm is an idiot."

"Not wise, my friend," said the tall man.

Rashid trembled. A wrong answer, and he knew he was a dead man—either by her hand or Saladin's. "I am not so foolish as to court death, Princess Badr al-Budur. I am here to help you."

"You are here for the reward."

"Yes," he answered. "But if I have nothing, you will give nothing."

"If you have nothing, I'll give you the point of my dagger," she said. "Or let Saladin break your arms and legs. Tell me what you know."

"I know a young baker," Rashid answered. "I knew him in Sidon when he was a merchant's son. Overnight he's become a baker in Al-Kal'as, one who feeds every beggar in sight."

The knife bit into his throat again. A second trickle of blood stained his jubba.

"I saw the lamp in his shop! It was tied to the waist of a girl, hidden beneath her robe."

"And what makes you think it was my lamp?" asked the Full Moon of Full Moons.

"I've been watching Hassan—the baker. He never buys flour or salt, yet he has fresh bread each day. He never buys charcoal or wood, yet his ovens are hot."

Badr withdrew the blade. "What has this to do with the girl?"

Rashid touched his neck, his fingers coming away red. "She visits Hassan often, in the dead of night. I listen to the murmur of their voices through the shutters. I never see her come or go, and she is never there in the morning. I laid eyes on her one night in Hassan's shop, when I went in to confront him. The doors were barred and yet she suddenly appeared. That's when I caught a momentary glimpse of the lamp swinging from her belt. Hassan told me she was his cousin Zubaydah—an obvious lie.

"After that, I began to ask myself questions. Could this be the beggar girl who stole the Princess's lamp? And why is the

Princess so anxious to retrieve an ordinary piece of brass? And what of Hassan and his amazing bakery?"

"Have you found answers?" asked Badr, sheathing the dagger.

Rashid could read in her eyes that she already knew the answers, but she expected to hear them from him. "You lost a magic lamp. Perhaps it holds a jinni, but that is none of my concern. Your lamp has given this girl power to appear and disappear at will. And given Hassan a way to bake without buying flour."

Badr dropped a bulging purse into his hand. "Tell me the way to this bakery."

When Rashid had finished describing the route, Saladin clapped his hands, and palace guards rushed back into the room.

"Take him away," their captain said.

"But Princess!" Rashid fell to his knees before Badr. "I told you the truth. I swear!"

"Knowledge is dangerous, little man," she said, "and you know too much."

Saladin laid his scimitar against Rashid's neck. "Speak another word, and it will be your last. Better a prison cell, don't you think?"

The Full Moon of Full Moons plucked the purse from Rashid's fingers as the guards pulled him away.

Fifth Moon

· Nineteen ·

"YOUR HEAD IS NOT IN THE GAME," said Jinni.

Aminah looked up from the chessboard. "What's that, Uncle Omar?"

"Check," he said, repositioning one of his horses. "This happened to me just yesterday when I was playing with Barra. My thoughts were elsewhere, as are yours. I almost lost the game to a novice."

"I can think of two things at once," she said, taking her king out of range. "So don't consider me an easy mark."

"Really?" He slid another piece forward. "Checkmate."

Aminah winced. "Morning isn't my best time for chess."

"It is afternoon," said Jinni.

"So it is," she answered, smiling. "You're right, of course. I can't concentrate because I've been worried about Hassan."

"Yes, I thought as much," he said. "Take care, Miss. You cannot afford to let matters of the heart cloud your judgment."

"Matters of the heart? Don't be ridiculous." Her laugh was nervous, unconvincing.

Jinni scowled. "You have feelings for this Hassan. That much is clear."

Aminah started to protest, then sighed. "Is it so obvious? I can't help it. When he takes my hand, I shiver. When he kisses me—"

"Kisses you!" Jinni turned purple. "Is this your idea of a

good deed, Miss? Outrageous! You need a father to take you in hand."

"Well, you're not my father. So don't try to tell me what to do with my life."

"Someone must protect you from such evils. Obviously your judgment is impaired."

"Evils? That's funny coming from a demon. And what do you mean my judgment is impaired?"

Jinni's scowl deepened. "You barely know this . . . this . . . I do not like you necking with some scruffy baker!"

"*Necking?*" Aminah asked. "*Scruffy?* Where do you come up with these bizarre words?"

"*Necking* means—" Jinni shook his head, a tight smile on his lips. "Never mind."

"What business is it of yours, anyhow?" Aminah demanded. "I'll kiss whom I please. I think this uncle business has gone to your head. Have you forgotten that you're the jinni and I'm the mistress of the lamp?"

The demon was silent, though steam billowed from his ears. He studied Aminah's face, almost as though she were a stranger.

"It's time I told you what I'm planning," she said. "We're leaving Al-Kal'as. I'll use my wishes to take us away: Barra, if she'll come, and Hassan, too. I doubt we'll have a chance to ask Idris."

"And why will you depart the city of your father's birth?" Jinni asked. He still examined her face so intently that he seemed to have forgotten their argument.

Ignoring his probing eyes, Aminah told him the story of Rashid's visit to the bakery. Jinni didn't seem surprised.

"I know Rashid took the money and agreed to go, but I don't trust him," she said.

"Ah, Rashid," Jinni said, finally lowering his gaze. "There is a man who confirms my beliefs about the human race."

"You speak as if you know him," said Aminah, an alarm going off inside her head.

"No, no, of course not. Only from your description."

"It was you!" Aminah cried. She jumped up and swept the chessboard to the floor, shattering it. "I can tell by the look on your scheming purple face!"

"I warned you, did I not? I told you if I helped with good deeds that no good would come of it."

"No, that's not what you said—not exactly. And you're wrong. What happened with Ahab was nothing if not good. What you should have said is that *you* would be the reason bad things would happen. You!" She shook her fist in Jinni's face. "You'll stay in the lamp from now on. You'll only see the outside world when I need to make wishes."

A shudder passed through Jinni. "I do not wish to displease you," he said.

"Then you'd better concentrate on getting us out of here when the wishing moon rises—unless you'd rather have Badr al-Budur ordering you about."

He shuddered again. "May I suggest you use the orb to spy on Rashid—and the Princess? That way you can stay several steps in the lead."

The fight seemed to go out of Aminah, and she sank back to her cushion. "I already tried, but the orb seemed confused—then went blank. Perhaps because I've only ever used it to find decent people like Ahab and Hassan. Hassan is decent, Jinni. You did a terrible thing."

"Yes," he said, glancing at the broken chessboard. Then his eyes locked on her face yet again. "I see that now, and it is odd to me that I do. It is not in the nature of jinn. Perhaps it is because of the vision."

"Vision?" asked Aminah.

"It happened again today—yet a stronger image than that with the horses. A vision of a different life, a human life. I am certain that I once played chess with another girl. Tonight I saw her face in yours, and I understood the terrible thing I have done to you."

"Jinni, I can almost forgive you."

The demon shook his head. "Be warned. This will likely pass when I am no longer caught in the vision's spell. But while it lasts, I wonder if the orb could find her," he said. "It can search the past."

"Then I will seek her for you," she said.

Jinni hesitated and then began tugging at his beard anxiously. "Another time, perhaps," he said. "Are you hungry?" he asked. "I could make you a pizza."

Aminah stared at Jinni in confusion. "You're hopeless! No, I'm not hungry, and I've never heard of pizza."

"No, of course not."

"What's the matter?" she asked. "Why have you changed your mind?"

"Please, Miss, I must return to the lamp."

"You're frightened, aren't you? Frightened of what you might discover."

"Please, allow me to return to the lamp," Jinni said again. "I must have time to think."

Aminah didn't argue, though she was intrigued about his vision of the past. The moment he disappeared, she took up the orb with the idea of finding the chess-playing girl. But when she touched the glass, it filled with a view of the bakery, and what she saw drove an icy spike into her chest.

The shop was in shambles. Shards of broken pottery littered the floor, along with splintered shelves and mangled utensils. Bread was cast about, and a blanket of flour and salt covered everything. The magic jars were gone.

Frantic, she manipulated the image in the orb, searching for Hassan. All she found were several small, dirty children picking through the rubble, salvaging the bread.

She sat back, her breath coming in shallow gasps, and tried to think. Was this the work of thieves? Had Rashid guessed Hassan's secret and come for the jars? Or was this the work of Badr and her palace guards?

Aminah closed her eyes and imagined a spot free of debris where the jars had once stood. Her fear intensified the effects of making the leap. Cold burned her cheeks and numbed her fingers. Her skin felt the prick of a thousand tiny needles, and she almost lost consciousness.

She landed in a heap on the bakery floor but couldn't remember falling. Struggling to focus her eyes, she saw small, dark shapes coming toward her. In a moment, she was surrounded by children who clutched scraps of bread to their thin chests. They stared at her with sunken eyes, unsurprised at her sudden appearance.

"Who did this?" she asked in a thick voice. "Who destroyed the shop?"

No one answered, and the children began backing away. But then a little girl stepped forward and leaned in close to Aminah. "Men from the palace, Miss," she whispered. "They took the baker away."

She reached out to the child, who shrank from her touch. The other children turned to run, and she slowly withdrew her hand. She understood their wariness; it had been part of her own survival instinct.

"Thank you," she said, holding out a dinar.

The girl darted forward, snatching the coin from her fingers and scampering out of reach again. "Something for my friends?" she asked, her dark eyes boring into Aminah.

"Yes," Aminah answered, and emptied her money belt into their grasping hands. She made certain the coins were divided equally among them, saving a few extra for the girl who had been bold enough to answer her question.

The children squealed in disbelief, holding the money high and darting from the bakery. Only the little girl stopped at the door. *"Alsalamu alaykum,"* she said. "And thank you." Then she fled after the others.

In an instant, Aminah was back in her room. Her skin mottled from the cold, she wrapped herself in a shawl and sat on the diwan. She allowed herself a few minutes to cry for Hassan—and for the children who needed his bread.

When she had gotten warm, Aminah dried her tears and threw off the shawl. Calm now, she took the orb in her hands and let her mind merge with its spirit. She pictured Hassan's strong features, his lovely features, and felt the orb probing the city to find him. She concentrated harder, her mind becoming the probe, and when the melding was complete, she set the scrying glass aside. The images flashed behind her eyelids now, and she directed herself toward the Sultan's palace.

She flew past the guards at the main gate and into the pavilion. For a moment, Aminah looked about in wonder at the polished marble floors, the soaring ceilings, and the gold that adorned every surface. Mosaics of hunting expeditions and desert oases and lush gardens covered the walls and were set not only with colored tiles but also with emeralds, rubies, and sapphires.

When she passed beneath the tallest belvedere, Aminah gazed upward in awe. Sunlight streamed through windows of colored glass and drenched her in a rainbow. The brightness almost blinded her mind's eye, and she hurried forward to clear her vision.

Aminah sensed that Hassan wasn't in the main palace or the living quarters, and so she ignored the kitchens, the council chambers, and the armory. Instead, she searched for the dungeon where the Sultan kept his prisoners. That seemed the more likely place to find him.

Leaving the splendor of the main rooms behind, she found a dark stone stairway leading downward. It ended in a wide tunnel carved from solid rock. She followed it to the left and came to a great iron door flanked by four guards with scimitars and spears gleaming in the lamplight.

She floated by the guards and through the heavy door. Four more guards stood before another portal, easing their boredom by sharing stories. Beyond that were four more guardsmen and yet another door—smaller, but every bit as solid.

There was only one man behind it—and endless chambers overflowing with the Sultan's treasure. Any one of the rooms held wealth enough to make a prince or princess of every beggar in Al-Kal'as.

Aminah traveled back the way she'd come. She passed the stairway and continued until the corridor ended at a small iron door with no one guarding it. As she drew near, she noticed a high, narrow window covered with a metal grate and peered through it. Inside, six men, hard-faced and muscular, lounged about in a dingy room. Four of them played at dice, while the other two manned the doors. Another portal, constructed of iron bars, stood on the far side of the chamber.

She floated through the iron plates and threaded her way among the jailers. But as she came even with the dicers, one of them cursed a bad throw. He leapt from the floor and into Aminah's path. She felt herself pass through him.

His friends mistook his strangled cry for poor sportsmanship and laughed, even when he sank to his knees. Aminah cried out at the same instant, her concentration broken, and she toppled backward onto the diwan.

She woke staring at the ceiling, her head throbbing. It was an hour before she was steady enough to try again. Ignoring the pain inside her skull, she gripped the orb. She screwed shut her eyes and fastened on Hassan's image, but nothing happened. She forced herself to relax, slowing her breathing, and envisioned the anteroom where the jailers were dicing.

For another hour, Aminah fought to connect with the orb, feeling its weak signals reaching out for her, but in the end, it was no use. She wondered if the orb, too, had been battered to the point of distress when she'd passed through the jailer's body. She was sure it would be back to normal by the next day or the one after that, but she couldn't wait.

Aminah knew the orb should have located Hassan within moments. That it had shown her the shattered bakery rather than his whereabouts could only mean that Hassan was either unconscious or . . . She shut her mind to the alternative and dressed in her magical thawb. Having learned to control the thawb, she willed it black as a starless, moonless night. She stood for a moment, ignoring the rash rising on her arms, and pictured the barred door at the far end of the jailers' anteroom. She'd seen a broad stone landing just beyond the bars, then a flight of stone stairs marching deeper into the earth. Aminah imagined herself on the landing, standing in the shadows.

· Twenty ·

THE COLD WASN'T AS BRUTAL this time, but Aminah still clenched her jaw to keep her teeth from chattering. She put out a hand to steady herself before peering around the doorway. The jailer she'd passed through lay on a pallet, still as a corpse, and Aminah felt a twinge of fear. Had she killed him? But then he moaned and turned over. His companions laughed, tossing the dice as if nothing was amiss, and she went limp with relief.

Behind her, prison cells lined the walls of a narrow passage that disappeared into the darkness. She heard men groaning and shifting in the blackness. At her feet, the stone stairs descended, and Aminah knew that more of the dungeon existed below.

She decided to look for Hassan on the lower levels, to put distance between her and the guards. She pulled the robe tightly around her and crept onto the steps, in full view of the jailers. But the stairway was in shadow, and the man rolling the dice held his companions' full attention. Aminah slipped out of sight, feeling for each step with her toes.

When she reached the bottom, she willed her thawb to shine with the soft light of a full moon. She shuddered, thinking of the men who huddled here in constant blackness, and cursed the Sultan. She wondered if Aladdin approved of his father-in-law's brand of justice, though she had little doubt about Badr's opinion.

In the thawb's light, Aminah saw corridors branching left and right from a main passage, some slanting yet farther into the earth. Cells lined each wall, and she hurried from one to the next, softly calling Hassan's name.

Men rose from fetid piles of straw, their eyes wide with fear. "A spirit," they murmured. "A demon." None dared raise his voice above a whisper.

The reek of filthy bodies and human excrement choked her. She covered her nose and pushed forward.

She came upon a chamber filled with strange devices, some the size of a large carpet loom. An array of dangerous-looking tools hung about the chamber, and a fire pit was hollowed from one wall. Dying coals winked from a brazier, wisps of smoke sucked into a flue carved from the rock. Aminah smelled something different in this place—the stench of old blood and burning flesh. Repulsed, she retreated into the passageway.

She traversed corridor after corridor, peering into cells, but no one answered her call. At last, she found herself back at the stairs. She doused the light in her thawb and was halfway up the steps when she froze. Loud voices approached the barred door, which banged open against the rock wall.

"Time to feed the goats," someone said.

Another voice laughed. "Not goats, Ali. Swine."

She fled down the stairs, her heart pounding in her ears. Buckets rattled in her wake, and feet thumped the stone steps. The noise panicked her, and Aminah forgot she could imagine herself home. Instead, she hurried to the only place where there were no prisoners to feed.

Afraid to light her way, she felt along the passages. How she remembered which turns to take, she didn't know, but somehow Aminah managed to find the torture chamber. She closed the iron door and crouched behind one of the loom-sized contraptions.

The embers in the brazier cast a weak amber glow. Aminah sat with her back to the wall, and in the dim light, she saw a small wooden door just beyond the fire pit. She thought it might lead to a better place to hide.

It swung open on silent hinges, and she stepped into the dark cavern, closing herself inside. Without outstretched hands, she discovered bars running along one wall and stifled a scream as something banged against the iron rods. She jumped back, lighting her thawb, and stared into Hassan's bloodied face.

Hassan stared back, his eyes glazed. He didn't seem to recognize her.

Aminah reached through the bars of the tiny cell, dabbing at the blood with her handkerchief. Then her eyes fell on his bare chest. The handkerchief dropped from her fingers, and she stepped back in horror. His flesh was scorched, the brands angry and weeping. He had been burned in at least a dozen places.

"I said nothing," he murmured and slipped to the floor, unconscious.

Aminah struggled to reach him and then remembered she could imagine herself inside the cell. In an instant she was there and knelt by him, cradling his battered head in her lap. She kissed his forehead, and his eyes fluttered open.

Hassan smiled, his lips cracking. "Aminah."

Choking back her sobs, she wrapped her arms around him

and made the leap back to her rooms, hoping he would travel with her. She arrived alone.

She flew back to him, and he smiled at her again. "Go from Al-Kal'as, Aminah," he said, though she had to lean close to hear him. "Go without me, or the Captain of the Guard will find you. The Princess . . ." His eyes rolled back in his head, and his body shuddered.

The door to the torture chamber crashed open, and Aminah jumped up.

"Delicacies," called a voice, followed by an ugly laugh. "Tidbits for the honored guest of Princess Badr al-Budur."

The jailer's bucket rapped against the wall as he pushed through the next door and into the room. Except for Hassan, his lamp revealed an empty cell.

Back in her quarters, Aminah swiped at her tears. What had she done? Instead of helping Hassan, she'd harmed him. She rubbed the lamp, and billowing purple smoke poured from it. The top of Jinni's head protruded from the cloud.

"Hassan is at death's door—all because of you!" Aminah cried.

"Use a wish," said Jinni. "We can save him."

Yes! A wish! Aminah had forgotten that the full moon was rising, and suddenly new hope swelled in her breast. "Get him out of there!" she screamed. "I want him out now!"

Jinni stepped from the cloud, dispersing it with a snap of his fingers. "Tell me where he is."

"The Princess has him! In the Sultan's dungeon."

The demon closed his eyes, searching the palace, and then snapped his fingers again. He disappeared into the lamp as Hassan, still as death, appeared at her feet. In the brighter light of her room, Aminah stared at his swollen face, dread creeping into her heart. She fell to her knees.

Hassan stirred as she slid his head into her lap. He opened his eyes and tried to sit up.

"Stay still," Aminah whispered. "You're safe."

"But . . . how . . . ?" he tried to ask.

"You'll know soon enough," she answered. "For now, let me tend your burns. And get some decent food into you."

Aminah moved Hassan to the diwan, then slipped from her quarters. First she went to Idris's room in the gardener's hut, which proved all but empty. *So,* she thought sadly, *he's taken his things. He won't be back.*

She poked through what he'd abandoned and found a few pieces of clothing to replace Hassan's. Then she moved to the kitchen. Barra was away, but Aminah managed to locate the ointment for burns, as well as fresh bandages. She took what food she could find, including some of Hassan's puffed-up bread and several cool sherbets, and hurried back to her quarters.

Tossing aside the clothing, Aminah knelt by Hassan and gently dabbed the ointment onto his burns. He winced, opening his eyes. He didn't seem as damaged as she'd feared.

"Sit up, if you can," she said.

With her help, he levered himself into a sitting position, groaning with the pain. Aminah bandaged his chest with wide swaths of white linen, then propped Hassan against several pillows.

"I hope you like your own bread," she said, laying out the food. "Here, drink this. I know you like banana-flavored sherbet."

She brought the glass to his lips, and he drank deeply before lying back on the pillows, his eyelids sagging. Aminah broke off pieces of the bread, dipping them in hummus, and fed him. He drank again and ate the fresh figs she offered him.

"Sorry I don't have more," she said. "It's all I could carry. Should I go back to the kitchen?"

Hassan shook his head and took her hand. He drew it to his face, kissing the tops of her fingers, and then laid her palm against his cheek. "Again, you save me," he said, his voice gaining strength. "Will I always be in your debt?"

"Most likely," she said.

Hassan laughed softly. "I am forever your slave," he said.

Aminah smiled. "Then I expect you to obey my orders." Her face grew solemn. "You must leave Al-Kal'as now. Tonight."

"The Princess will be watching every gate."

"But you won't be leaving through any of the gates."

He looked puzzled. "You want me to drop over the wall?"

Aminah sighed. "It's time you knew the truth. As I told you, my father was once a scholar in the palace. I'd hoped that would earn me a little consideration when I tried begging at the Princess's balcony. Instead, she threw an old, battered oil lamp at me and struck me in the forehead." She touched her scar.

Hassan's lip curled. "Ever a sweet spirit, the Full Moon of Full Moons."

"It was Aladdin's lamp, and what the Princess didn't know was that it held a jinni."

His eyes widened.

"That golden ducat Rashid spotted in the sand—part of my first wish. I get three wishes with every full moon."

"I take it the Princess now knows about the jinni," said Hassan.

Aminah nodded.

"I won't leave without you."

"Yes, my slave, you will. Put these on," she said, tossing him Idris's clothes. "I know you're weak, but there isn't time for resting."

She left him to change, ignoring his protests, and went into her sleeping quarters to get the lamp.

"Where would you like to go?" Aminah asked.

Hassan slipped on Idris's old jubba and said, "Not home. There's nothing left for me there."

"I'm sending the jars, too. And as long as I possess the lamp, the power to heat ovens will be yours. That means any oven will do. I hope you'll set up shop and keep on feeding people. So where will it be?"

He thought a moment. "How about Tyre? I want to see the place where you swam. I'll try it myself before you come. You will come, won't you?"

Aminah smiled. "Yes. I'll come as soon as I can. Now it's time for you to meet Jinni."

She rubbed the lamp, and Jinni catapulted from the midst of a soundless purple explosion, towering over them and wearing one of his most frightening faces. Hassan cried out and fell back onto his pillows, clutching his sore chest.

"Jinni!" Aminah's glare took the steam out of the purple giant, and he shrank into Uncle Omar.

"My apologies," he said, bowing to Hassan. "It is not often I get the opportunity to do that these days. I could not resist."

Hassan stared, speechless.

"You don't look sorry at all," said Aminah. "But never mind that—we haven't the time. I wish to send the jars—wherever they are—and Hassan to Tyre. Can I do that with one wish?"

Jinni shook his head. "The Princess has the jars, and you may send them from the palace to Tyre, but it will take another wish to send the baker."

"Then my three wishes will be used," she said, reaching for Hassan's hand. "I'd hoped to have one left over to heal your burns."

"They'll heal on their own," Hassan said. "Don't worry."

Seeing them stand hand in hand, Jinni scowled. "I warn you, baker, I will cause you a thousand times more trouble than your friend Rashid. Hear me, baker—"

"His name is Hassan," Aminah interrupted. "You seem to remember Rashid's name easily enough."

Jinni glared at her. "Hear me, baker. Do not trifle with this girl. If you have designs on the lamp, you had best forget them. I will be a danger to you, even as your slave."

"Jinni!" Aminah stamped her foot. "Stop that!"

The demon's face darkened. "Hearing and obeying," he growled.

"No!" she cried. "That wasn't a wish! Don't do this to me."

Jinni shrugged. "I have done nothing but fulfill your requests. I tried looking out for you, but it appears my efforts are not trusted—or wanted. You have one wish left, Miss."

Tears filled Aminah's eyes. "I thought you cared about me . . . at least a little."

His hard look softened for a moment.

"Go away!" she cried, her cheeks wet. "Go back to the lamp."

Eyes downcast, Jinni snapped his fingers, and two things happened in an instant. First, he turned to smoke and was sucked into the lamp's narrow spout with such force that the air was filled with a bone-chilling shriek. Second, Hassan's fiery red jars materialized about the room.

· Twenty-one ·

AMINAH WASN'T SURE what the appearance of the jars meant, and she was still too hurt and furious to summon Jinni for an explanation. She told Hassan she needed to think before calling the demon back. By the time he'd fallen asleep again, the edge was off her pain and anger.

She left Hassan on the diwan and tiptoed into her bedroom, closing the door. She stroked the lamp and stood back while a fine violet mist flowed from the spout. Jinni took shape within the vapor.

"I cannot undo what has been done," he said, before Aminah could speak. "Petty of me, to be sure, but once I have granted a wish—"

"I didn't ask for the jars," she interrupted, her face rigid as flint. "Have you tricked me into using my third wish? Jinni, so much is at risk. Are you so heartless?"

"I am a demon. Have you forgotten? Place your hand on my chest, if you want. You will feel no heart beating inside."

"How could I have let myself be fooled?" Aminah fought back her tears. "How could I have seen anything of my father in you?"

Jinni's eyebrows flew up in surprise. "I reminded you of your father?"

"Perhaps a little—only sometimes."

"Well now," he said, still looking surprised. "The jars should not stay in the possession of the Full Moon of Full Moons. I brought them here for safekeeping. This was not one of your wishes, Aminah."

"Perhaps you should call me Miss," she said, looking away. "So why bring the jars here? Wouldn't they be safer in . . . in demon country where no one can get to them? If you've done this as a peace offering, then it's an empty gesture. I still can't send both the jars and Hassan to Tyre with one wish."

"Oh?" said Jinni.

His tone brought Aminah's head around. "*Is* there a way, Jinni? There is! I can see it in your eyes."

"I cannot send both the jars and Hassan, as I have already told you. That would require two wishes," he said. "However, if the vessels were filled with flour or oil, the contents would travel quite nicely with them."

"Stop changing the subject! Who cares if full jars . . . wait a minute. You don't mean . . ."

Jinni nodded, then began to laugh.

"What's so funny?" Aminah demanded.

"Two dozen guards," he said, holding his sides. "Running willy-nilly looking for the jars. Banging into walls. Cursing and beating one another for falling asleep on the job. Oh, it was rich!"

☽

HASSAN STEPPED FORWARD and encircled Aminah in his arms. He couldn't hold her close because of his burns, so he leaned forward to kiss her. Jinni's face tightened, but he said nothing.

She handed Hassan a purse heavy with gold—the last of the ducats. "To get you started. And for the land. The hilltop overlooking the sea, remember?"

He smiled. "Yes, but how long will it be before we can stand there together?"

"We'll come by caravan. You know how slow that can be. I'll have to sell the house, and then we'll leave. If we were to go right away, so soon after your disappearance from the palace, we'd raise suspicions. It may be six months or more."

Hassan sighed. "I hope I can bear to be away from you so long."

Aminah started to cry. "I'm pretending to be strong about this," she stammered, "but I . . . I can't manage it. Go now, or it will only get harder."

Their parting kiss was long and deep, and as Jinni watched, a faint smile played about his lips. At last, with a gentle nudge, Aminah pushed Hassan away.

"Go," she said.

With painful reluctance, Hassan moved to the tallest of the jars, and, standing on a stool, hoisted himself up and over the rim. He disappeared inside, but his voice, ringing hollow, rose through the opening. "I love you."

"I love you, too," Aminah answered, her voice choked with emotion. Then she steeled herself and turned to Jinni. "I wish these jars in Tyre. Deposit them in the courtyard of the best kahn in the city, without anyone noticing their arrival, of course."

"Of course. Do you not think I know my work?" Jinni said, trying to sound testy. "Close thine eyes and open thine eyes, and it shall be as thou commandeth."

Not questioning Jinni's flowery formalities, Aminah squeezed her eyes tightly shut. "Good-bye, Hassan," she whispered.

)

THE NEXT MORNING DAWNED warm and dusty, announcing the sizzling heat to come. Barra weeded a portion of the flower bed that fell in a palm tree's shadow. She knew nothing about Hassan and so waved cheerily when Aminah stepped from her quarters.

"Up so early?" she asked.

"I've been up for hours—before the sun," said Barra. "Shall we breakfast?"

Aminah nodded. As she locked arms with Barra and strolled toward the kitchen, she realized the magic in her life had only a little to do with the wishing moon. A mother, a true love—those were her enchantments. *And Idris,* she thought with regret.

Later in the day, she called on Jinni. "I'll offer the house for sale tomorrow. Maybe we can leave sooner than I told Hassan," she said to him, "depending on when a caravan leaves for Tyre."

"I will await your decision," he said.

"I'm tired, Jinni," said Aminah. "I don't know if I can do this anymore."

"Now it is you who speaks in riddles, Miss."

"Being mistress to a jinni, I mean—much less friends with one. It's too unpredictable."

"I have given you reason not to trust me," Jinni said, "but do not think I mean you harm. And now the same is true for Hassan."

She shrugged. "We'll talk in Tyre. That will give me the time I need to think this through."

Jinni bowed. "As you wish."

Aminah smiled. "I've no wishes to lose so, yes, it's what I wish. I'll call for you again soon."

Issuing a forlorn salute in her direction, Jinni dissolved and was drawn into the lamp.

She stood for a moment, watching the last of him drift away, then opened the hidden compartment and set the lamp on the shelf. Her eyes fell on Hassan's water skin, and her own melancholy deepened. She reached for the skin, hugging it to her breast, but was distracted by Barra's voice calling from outside.

"Zubaydah? May . . . may I see you?"

Barra's voice quavered, and Aminah dropped the water skin at the sound. Something was wrong. Had she injured herself in the kitchen?

Aminah rushed to the door, throwing it open to the courtyard. "Barra—"

Surrounded by palace guards, Barra stood frozen, the tip of a guardsman's knife at her throat. Princess Badr al-Budur stepped from behind them, her dark eyes laughing.

"Meet Saladin, Captain of the Guard," she said. The tall man holding Barra smiled.

"I hear you come and go rather mysteriously," Badr continued. "Try it, and the woman dies."

Aminah stepped outside, pulling the door closed behind her, and moved into the sunlight.

"You shouldn't have used your aunt's name, Aminah," said the Princess. "Not very bright, for a scholar's daughter."

"Was it Rashid?" Against her will, Aminah's voice trembled.

"Yes, as a matter of fact. He mentioned the baker's cousin, Zubaydah. It didn't take long to piece things together, with help from the man who sold you this place—it's quite nice, by the way, for a beggar girl's. However, we should have figured it out months ago." She shot Saladin a murderous look. "I'm quite displeased with my spies."

"I feel sorry for them."

The Princess laughed. "You know me well."

"The Sultan must be proud of his little girl," said Aminah, trying to sound bold. "And Aladdin of his wife."

"Father doesn't pay me any mind. And Aladdin . . . Well, I suppose it won't hurt to tell you that my plans don't include either of them," she said. "I've enjoyed visiting, Aminah— though I don't spend time with paupers as a rule. Now, let's get on with business. Give me the lamp."

Aminah gazed in the air above Badr's head, weighing her own life against Barra's. Once she gave up the lamp, her magic was finished. The Princess would kill her.

Saladin's blade drew blood, and Barra screamed.

"Stop!" Aminah slumped against a palm tree, shaking.

"Only if you take me to the lamp," said the Full Moon of Full Moons.

She nodded, staring in a daze at the Princess. Badr was the ideal of Arabian beauty: a figure slim as bamboo, yet with wide hips and breasts like pomegranates; large dark eyes set in a full-moon face; hair blacker than ink; a small mouth filled with shining teeth; even a beauty mark dotting her face like a drop of ambergris. As she moved toward her quarters, Aminah said, "Your beauty hides a dark heart."

Badr laughed again. "It is the heart of a Sultan—your Sultan, though you may not live to see me rule. Remember, the woman dies if you disappear. She also dies if you disappear after I possess the lamp. Is that clear?"

Aminah nodded.

Within her quarters, she hesitated again. What if Badr was bluffing? After the Princess took the lamp but before she had a chance to become Jinni's mistress, Aminah could leap to Tyre. With the lamp in hand, the Full Moon of Full Moons wouldn't have a reason to kill anyone.

Barra whimpered from behind her, and Aminah was forced to admit the truth. Badr did have a reason—hatred for the beggar girl who'd shamed her. At the same time, Aminah realized she could never risk Barra's life. No one—especially Barra—would die because of her. With grim resignation, she led Badr to the door of the hidden room, which still stood open.

Aminah fell back with a gasp. The shelves were empty. She turned wild eyes on the Princess. "But it was here!" she cried.

"Kill the woman," said Badr.

Saladin pulled back Barra's head. She fell against him, sobbing, and he raised his knife with a flourish.

"No!" Aminah screamed.

Time seemed to slow as the blade sliced through her throat, and then Barra dropped to the floor, making a hideous gurgling sound. Aminah turned away.

"She's hidden it somewhere else," said Badr. "Take her back to the courtyard."

Saladin waved a guard forward. Rough hands closed on her arms, and she was forced toward the door. The guard had taken only a few steps when his bruising grasp released her. Aminah stood for a moment, then whirled around.

Saladin was gone. All the guards were gone, and so was Badr al-Budur.

Sixth Moon

· Twenty-two ·

AMINAH HURRIED to Barra's still form. She turned her over, and the sobs died in Aminah's throat. Dumbstruck, she searched for the gaping hole in the woman's neck. Not even a scar was visible, and the ruddiness in Barra's cheeks belied what Aminah had witnessed—blood gushing from an ugly wound.

Befuddled by what had just happened to Barra—and to Badr and her henchmen—Aminah could only think of their getting away from the house. But before she could pull Barra to her feet, a shadow fell across the threshold. She froze, staring at the doorway, until a face peered around the edge.

"Uncle Omar?" Aminah was stunned.

Jinni stepped into the room. Idris followed, holding the lamp.

"He insisted on coming with me," said Idris, grinning.

"I'll deal with you two in a minute," Aminah said in a quavering voice. Then, eyes averted from the hideous red stain on the carpet, she led Barra into her bedroom.

Dazed, Barra didn't speak. She curled up on the bed and fell into a deep sleep the moment her head touched the pillow. Aminah sat for a while, watching the slow rise and fall of the woman's chest, and suddenly realized that her wish on Barra's behalf—the wish for a long life—had been what had saved her. She reached for Barra's limp hand and pressed it to her cheek. Then she kissed away the grateful tears that had spilled from her eyes onto the cook's rough skin.

Aminah crept from the bedchamber and found Jinni alone, pacing the floor. Before she could ask after Idris, he came from outside, carrying her chest of gold coins and Hassan's water skin. A bulge in the pocket of his jubba revealed the orb.

"I buried them under the horses' feed," he said. "Then we came looking for you."

Aminah scanned the room for the lamp and found it sitting next to the shattered remains of the chessboard. Idris followed her eyes. "Quite an amazing bauble," he said.

She crossed to Idris and embraced him. "You knew about the lamp all along, didn't you?"

"And fortunate for us he did," said Jinni. "Aladdin was not such a bad master, but the thought of Badr al-Budur . . ." He shivered, turning a dirty shade of purple.

"I'm afraid I spied on you," said Idris.

"And fortunate for us he did," Jinni repeated.

"I am sorry," Idris said. "But not too sorry. I'd do the same thing again, if it meant saving your neck."

Aminah automatically put a hand to her throat, thinking of Barra. "Your timing was just right. If you'd called on Jinni a few moments earlier, Barra would be dead now. The moment you rubbed the lamp, the protection spell I'd wished for her was gone."

The look on Idris's face was a mixture of horror and bewilderment.

"Don't worry. I'll explain everything as soon as Barra wakes up, and then you'll understand," said Aminah. "No more secrets. I should have trusted you from the beginning, Idris. Instead, I forced you to spy on me. And to leave us."

Idris smiled. "I almost slipped and called you Aminah more than once."

Her mouth fell open. "You knew my real name, too?"

"It's the least a good spy ought to have discovered," he said.

"Don't I feel the fool," said Aminah. "And I think it's only going to get worse when you tell me the rest. What happened to the Princess?"

"New master, new wishes," said Jinni. "The Princess has been bewitched."

Aminah bowed to Idris. "Hail, new master of the lamp."

"Oh, you can have it back," he said. "I never meant to keep it. Besides, I've had enough of magic."

"Enough of magic? Insult and ingratitude!" cried Jinni. "However, the boy has two wishes left, and you may as well let him use them. Even if you take back the lamp, it will do you no good until the next full moon. By the way, only three different masters are allowed each month—relatives do not qualify."

Aminah laughed. "I suppose that makes sense. How did you get the lamp, Idris? And the rest of the things? Were you hiding in here?"

"This is the good part," said Jinni.

Idris shifted uncomfortably. "I rigged one of your window screens before I left to stay with my friend, the storyteller—the window away from the courtyard. I wanted a way to reach you if the door was locked and there was trouble."

"And fortunate for us he did," said Jinni.

"Don't tell me," Aminah said. "A good spy could do no less."

"That's right." Idris grinned. "I've been keeping a sharp eye on the place. When I saw the Princess and her thugs coming from a distance—well, I have a way over the wall, a spot where no one can see me. I was in and out of your quarters not a moment too soon. It helped that the vault door was open. An extra few seconds to undo the lock and Badr would've had me."

"This is too much!" Aminah cried. "You found out my combination of symbols? How?"

"A professional secret," Idris said, suddenly uneasy.

"A professional secret named Uncle Omar, I'd guess." She could tell by Jinni's wandering eyes that she was right. "So, Master of the Lamp, what did you do with the Princess?"

"I sent her to Makkah—or, rather, Jinni did. I thought she needed a little religion."

"You didn't! She'll be forever getting home. All the guards, too?"

Idris nodded. "Do you think she'll do the hajj while she's there? I've given her a real opportunity."

"Somehow I don't think the Princess will be in the mood for a pilgrimage. Besides, she'd have to wait around for several months for the hajj to begin." She turned to Jinni. "If you can send a crowd away with one wish, why not jars and people?" She struggled to keep an accusing tone from her voice.

"Minor rule number five hundred twelve *A*," Jinni answered. "I may move things by classes. People together. Jars together. Horses together. I simply had to exclude you and Barra. Minor rule number five hundred twelve *B* allows anything inside a container to be moved with the container. Bakers in a jar. The entire contents of this house. Even a whole city inside a city wall."

"How do you keep all these rules straight?" Idris asked.

"Photographic memory," he said.

"What?"

"Never mind."

"One of Jinni's many strange words," said Aminah. "One gets used to them and simply stops paying attention."

"Pizza. Buick. IBM. Eiffel Tower," Jinni said, frowning at her. "Boeing seven forty-seven, Australia, Elvis Presley, baseball—"

"Enough!" she cried, laughing. "By the way, Idris, if you know so much, can you tell me when a caravan leaves for Tyre?"

"As a matter of fact, I can. There's one going in two weeks. You'll be with Hassan soon enough—and I think it's high time. I acted like a pig, Aminah. Forgive me?"

Aminah's eyes glistened. "I want you to come with us, Idris."

His expression softened. "I hoped you'd ask. It means a great deal to me, though I won't be coming along."

"But why?"

"I have a dream to follow, at least for a while."

"Storytelling," said Aminah.

Idris nodded, his eyes shining. "Captivating an audience, Aminah! It's intoxicating. And I'm getting very good at it. Who knows, one day I might appear in Tyre, telling tales in the suq."

"And perhaps when your traveling is done, you'll come home."

"Perhaps," said Idris.

"Pardon me," Jinni interrupted. "Are you humans hungry, by chance?"

"Yes! As hungry as I've ever been," said Aminah. "Idris, why don't you send your jinni to see what he can find?"

When Jinni was gone, an uncomfortable stillness filled the room.

"This is silly," said Aminah. "Can't we keep talking without Jinni around? And speaking of Jinni, I'd be careful with your next two wishes. He's tricked me into bad choices more than once."

"Oh, I'm not worried. He's a fellow horse lover, after all." But then Idris paused, a troubled look crossing his face. "What about the horses? Will you take them with you?"

"They're yours," she said.

Idris smiled. "Thank you."

"However, I will expect to see your stallions again—in Tyre, of course. Let's go visit them. I won't have many more chances."

When she and Idris returned from the stables, Jinni had laid out food from one end of the quarters to the other. On an embroidered cloth in the center of the room lay meat pies and bowls of dates, figs, and fresh fruit—apricots, grapes, oranges. On several low tables were silver trays bearing sweetmeats, bowls of almonds and olives, and ewers of sherbet and yoghurt drink.

"A celebration," he said, spreading his arms wide.

Aminah joined Idris in picking through the delicacies. She pretended to ignore Jinni, who stood watching with a long face. Then she leaned close and whispered in Idris's ear. "He can't eat unless you invite him."

Idris looked up from the feast "You there. Demon," he said, smiling at the unhappy jinni. "Eat your fill."

Jinni threw himself on a meat pie like a wild dog on a rabbit carcass. Idris looked on in amazement—and disgust.

Barra awoke and joined them as the meal drew to a close. She hugged Idris, and then surveyed the mess in dismay. She insisted on cleaning up, but Aminah made her sit down. Idris brought her a tray, but she only picked at it out of duty, touching her neck all the while. Afterward, Aminah led her back to bed. Jinni and Idris tidied the room without the benefit of magic.

"Is your name really Aminah?" Barra asked, when they were alone.

She nodded.

"What happened? Why am I still breathing?"

Aminah sat down next to Barra and took her hand. "I have so much to tell you."

>)

WHEN THE SUN HAD SET behind the distant hills, Aminah brought everyone together on the rooftop terrace so they could enjoy the fresh breezes that banished the day's oppressive heat. Jinni was perched on a low stool, drinking from a tall glass of sherbet. Barra and Idris sat next to each other on thick, bright-colored carpets. Aminah folded herself onto a rug, as well, while Barra threw nervous glances at Jinni. She was still unused to the idea of a demon loose in the house—especially one she'd taken a liking to.

"We can be sure the Sultan has begun searching for his daughter, so I think we should leave right away," said Aminah. "I thought at first it would be better to wait, but that was when I thought Badr would be looking for Hassan."

"And now she's a thousand leagues away," said Idris.

"Thanks to me, of course," said Jinni, inflating his chest.

"I planned to go by caravan," Aminah continued. "But now

a long, roasting trip across the desert isn't necessary. Actually, it never was. According to minor rule number five hundred twelve B, I could have taken the entire house to Tyre when I sent Hassan—with all of us inside."

"Except you would have missed seeing Idris," Barra reminded her.

Aminah nodded. "Yes, so I suppose it really did work out for the best. And now Jinni can whisk us off to Tyre, anyway."

"But that means waiting a month for your next wishing moon," said Barra.

"It's not my moon," said Aminah. "But the current owner still has two wishes, and it would require only one. If we stood inside the stable, then Jinni could send us and our things all at once."

"Why not use the house instead?" asked Jinni. "I could drop the whole place on that seaside hill you love so much."

"If a house like this appeared in an instant, it would be the talk of Tyre. No, it's better if our arrival isn't noticed."

"I think I'd rather go by caravan," said Barra, who cast another anxious glance at Jinni. "Magic can poison the heart, as it did with the Princess. Perhaps it is best left alone."

"It's not the magic that poisons," said Aminah. "The venom is already in one's heart, I think. In the right hands, good may come of it, too. Why, magic brought us together, when you think about it."

Barra smiled. "Do I hear the wisdom of Allah? Is this the same little dove?"

Aminah laughed. "Was I so foolish?"

"No," Barra answered. "The magic you worked in Ahab's life—and in Hassan's—that was anything but foolish."

"Ahab!" Aminah clutched Jinni's sleeve. "His powers are gone, aren't they? And Hassan's?"

Jinni nodded. "Ahab still has Khalidah, but that is all. And Hassan still has the jars, but no power to heat ovens. It is the same with your ability to travel through space and time. Of course, you retain the money box—and orb, though I suppose it ought soon to go back to the wizard."

Aminah turned to Idris. "I need your wishes," she said, her voice desperate. "Please."

"I thought I'd save one for me," he said. "Perhaps a money box like yours that never empties. That would be quite useful for a poor traveling storyteller. Or maybe fame—the most renowned spinner of tales in the world!"

Aminah looked at the floor to hide her disappointment. It was only natural that Idris should want to use a wish. Besides, he deserved that much of a reward. When she looked up again, she saw Idris shrug.

"Oh bother," he said. "If I don't earn my own fame, it isn't really fame at all, is it? And a money box would just weigh me down."

Aminah hugged him gratefully. "Ask Jinni to return Ahab's gift for tailoring. He must think I've abandoned him."

"Jinni, if you can put down that glass long enough, I want to make a wish," Idris said.

"I am not deaf," Jinni retorted. "I know what is wanted. Still, you must say it."

"All right. I wish to restore Aminah's wish for Ahab the tailor—the one that gives him magical tailoring skills."

Jinni stood, burping loudly, and crossed his arms. "SO BE IT!" he roared.

The house shook beneath them. Cries of "Earthquake!" rose from the streets and surrounding buildings.

"Oops," said Jinni, looking smug. "I forgot. No longer ruled by your 'quiet wish,' am I, Miss?"

"Jinni, you're incorrigible," said Aminah, shaking her head. "A wish for Hassan, Idris, and then I'm finished. The lamp will be yours. You can wait a month for a money box, can't you?"

In the midst of pouring himself yet another sherbet, Jinni slammed down the pitcher. "If you hand me over to the boy, he will regret the day he laid eyes on me," his demon voice rumbled. He couldn't seem to contain himself, swelling to three times human size. A deep, angry shade of purple filled his body and a viscous, plum-colored fluid dripped from his ears and nostrils. "Every wish he makes will come to misery! Destruction! Anguish!"

"It's this kind of behavior that has wearied me," said Aminah, putting a hand out to still Barra's quaking. "You're not reliable, and I shouldn't expect it. You're a demon, after all, not my uncle. I need a rest. Let Idris take a turn."

Jinni shook his head. Instantly, he reverted back to Omar.

"I don't want the lamp," said Idris. "If I use the third wish for Hassan—which I must say is asking a lot of me—then how will you get to Tyre? And if I send you to Tyre, then I'm stuck with the lamp. I don't like any of the choices."

Jinni cleared his throat. "Pardon me, Master. I have a suggestion." His subservient tone was something new, and the others looked at him in surprise.

"The lamp can have three masters in a month, if you recall." Jinni spoke in such a humble voice that Aminah almost laughed. "Barra could be number three—temporarily, of course."

"How about it, Barra?" Idris asked. "I'll give Aminah another wish, and then you make the wish for Tyre."

Barra hesitated. "Fine, I'll do it. But Aminah's getting that piece of demon brass back the second the full moon rises. A caravan sounds better all the time."

"I suppose it's settled, then," said Aminah. "Except the part about me getting back the lamp. Idris, would you return Hassan's intuition for baking—and his power for heating ovens?"

"I am sorry, but that is two wishes." Jinni bowed with what seemed like true regret. "If it were up to me, I would combine them, but the Powers . . ."

This time Aminah did laugh. "This is a whole new side of you, Jinni. If Barra doesn't mind, we'll use her first wish to finish up with Hassan."

Barra nodded.

"With all respect, let me ask you to hurry," Jinni said. "I am beginning to feel odd. The effects of doing good deeds are lurking, ready to pounce."

Idris quickly made his wish for Hassan. Jinni followed with a subdued "So be it" and then disappeared into the lamp.

"Come back!" cried Idris. "We're not done with you."

"It's his habit to return to the lamp after a third wish," said Aminah. "I only hope he's not too sick to be summoned again. Your turn, Barra."

Barra's palms were sweating as she reached for the lamp. With a disgusted snort, she stroked the lid with one finger, and Jinni's purple head burst from the spout.

"Boo!" he cried.

She screamed, dropping the lamp.

"What's gotten into you?" Idris demanded.

The demon pulled the rest of himself from the spout, then sang in a high-pitched voice: "So many masters so quickly, sure to make a jinni tipsy." He giggled, staggering as if he'd had too much wine. "I feel magnifious! So magnifious that even doing good deeds cannot bring me down! Hooray! Hurrah! Huzzah!"

"Back to the lamp, Jinni," said Aminah. "You're scaring me."

"No, no. You are no longer the Master, Mistress. She be the one," he said, bending in a deep bow to Barra and toppling over. He crawled back to his feet. "Your command is my wish, you pretty little thing."

"You're drunk," said Barra, shaking a finger at him and blushing at the same time. "I haven't been pretty in at least a dozen years—well, perhaps half a dozen."

"Make the wish," Aminah said. "And remind him to be quiet."

"I wish for you to return to Hassan the power to heat his ovens," she said, glaring at the swaying jinni. "And be quiet about it."

Jinni put a finger to his lips. "I am the hand between thy slaves," he whispered. "Be so it!"

· Twenty-three ·

JINNI WAS IN SUCH A STATE that he didn't argue about returning to the lamp after granting Barra's wish. The following day, Aminah suggested Barra try summoning him again and wasn't surprised when he didn't appear.

It was two days before Jinni responded to a summons, and then only his feeble voice drifted from the spout. On the third day, he managed to squeeze himself from the lamp. He stood on wobbly legs, a grimace on his pale purple face.

"Madam, I am sorry for not being myself with you," he said to Barra.

"Not yourself?" she said. "You were a drunken lout!"

Jinni gave her a rueful smile. "I did not intend it."

"Not that you're interested," said Aminah, "but I used the orb to look in on Hassan. He's back in business and is healing well."

"Your face glows with the fire of a thousand candles when you speak his name," said Jinni.

"Only a thousand, Jinni? Surely a hundred thousand. A thousand thousand."

"A million thousand, I'd say," said Barra. "Do you think she's in love?"

"Of course I'm in love, and seeing Hassan without being able to touch him was agony! Will we be ready to leave by tomorrow?"

"You'd better be," said Idris. "Or you'll burst into a thousand thousand pieces."

"Are you making fun of me?" she asked.

"I would never do that," Idris answered, with a grin.

"By the way, I saw Ahab, too. His skills are back in working order, and he and Khalidah have forty-five children now."

"Forty-five!" Idris shook his head. "They'll have a hundred in no time."

"Yes," said Jinni. "Some would say Ahab's accomplishments have been a decent exchange for a few days of jinni discomfort. Hassan's, as well."

"And what would *you* say, Jinni?" asked Aminah.

"I say that it was an honor to serve you, Miss."

"Who are you?" she asked, eyeing him dubiously. "Idris, someone has stolen our old jinni and substituted this one."

❯

AMINAH ASKED Barra's permission to visit with Jinni that evening, their last evening in Al-Kal'as. He'd arrived at her door looking like Uncle Omar and, at Aminah's suggestion, magically repaired the broken chessboard. Now they sat across the board from one another in deep concentration. Aminah made a move, then sat back and said, "Thank you for suggesting that Barra use the lamp. It was decent of you to see that things were fixed for both Ahab and Hassan. It almost makes me sad to be giving you over to Barra."

"But the woman does not want me, that is plain to see," Jinni answered. "Barra has no use for magic, and she plans to give the lamp back to you. Please take it."

Aminah smiled. "I do believe you like me, after all. But no, I think it's for the best if Barra takes the lamp. At least for a time."

"You will change your mind," he said. "Of that I am confident."

She smiled again and shook her head. "However, I don't need the lamp to help you find out who you are. I think it's time, Jinni."

He reached for a sweetmeat from a nearby platter. "This is very good," he said. "Perhaps the best we have had. What do you think?"

"You're trying to change the subject."

"Some say changing the subject is my best bit of magic," said Jinni.

Aminah laughed. "Then tell me about Galileo and New York City and pizza."

Jinni chewed slowly and swallowed. "You have a good memory, Miss."

"Are you going to tell me or not?"

"Jinn can travel through time, or at least, see into time. I particularly like the future."

"You already told me Galileo was from the future. New York City, too?"

"Yes, but it will not be for a thousand years. New Yorkers have wonderful pizza. Pizza is food—a disk made of bread, tomato sauce, cheese, pepperoni . . ." His face took on a dreamy look.

"You've tasted it?" she asked.

"No. But I am certain I would love it."

Aminah was ready to ask about pepperoni when she had a staggering thought. "You can see back in time, Jinni!"

"That is true."

"Don't you understand? You could look back and find out about yourself."

"Jinn are not allowed."

"Then break the rules."

"It is not a matter of breaking rules. I cannot visit my own past. It is not possible." He plucked another sweetmeat from the tray.

"Then use the orb. You wanted to once before."

Jinni sighed. "I cannot. The orb will not show me my own past."

"But I already offered to search for you." She pulled the orb from her pocket.

"This is why you brought me here tonight?" he asked.

"Yes, I suppose so. But I did want to play chess, too. I hoped the game would signal a truce between us. Come, let's look into the orb together."

Jinni brushed the crumbs from his fingers and stood, his face draining of color.

"I must go," he said.

"Why?" Aminah asked, but his body was already smoke.

As the vapors trailed across the windowsill, drifting toward Barra's room and the lamp, Jinni's voice whispered, and she strained to catch the words. "You would not be successful if I stayed."

Aminah somehow knew he was right, but she felt abandoned. "Perhaps it would be better if I left this alone," she wondered aloud, then pushed aside her doubts.

She closed her eyes, stroking the orb, and felt herself slipping inside its consciousness, merging with it in the same way as when she'd searched the palace for Hassan. Soon images flashed inside her head, and she set the scrying glass aside.

Aminah spiraled back through time, her mind probing the crimson mists that clouded the past, reaching out for the person Jinni had been. Then in what seemed like an instant—or perhaps it was hours—there he was.

She had no doubts she'd found him. He looked exactly like the younger version of Uncle Omar, except that his eyes were harder, his face slier. Her stomach tightened, and she wondered again if she should have left this alone.

The young man sat with a girl, playing chess—the image that had flickered across Jinni's memory. Aminah watched the girl scowl over her next move, her pretty face puckering. She made her move and laughed. It was the sound of pure and innocent joy.

"I've trapped you, Gindar!" she cried, spreading her arms wide. "Checkmate!"

"Indeed, little sister," said Gindar. His eyes softened when he looked at her. "I've taught you too well."

Aminah was relieved. He seemed kind. Perhaps he couldn't help the hard look in his eyes.

"Put up the board and chess pieces, Jamila," he said. "I have business in the city."

Jamila took hold of her brother's sleeve. "Thank you for playing," she said.

Gindar smiled and kissed her forehead.

He left the room, and Aminah followed him into the streets. She soon discovered they were walking through the ancient city of Al-Hirah. But no one acknowledged Gindar as he passed. Instead, people turned their heads or ducked into alleys to avoid him. Then he came to a bakery, not unlike Hassan's in Al-Kal'as. The happy chatter inside stopped as he entered.

"Peace be with you," said the nervous baker, bowing to Gindar.

"I am calling in your debt, Amin," he said. "Pay now, or I will take your shop."

Amin groveled and begged, but Gindar only laughed. "I am a generous man," he said. "You may have until tomorrow at this time."

"But my children!" cried Amin. "Will you toss them into the streets?"

"Your children are not my concern," said Gindar. "I'll have my money, baker. Tomorrow."

Aminah saw the same scene repeated more than once that day. Each time Gindar's eyes glittered with greed. At last, she followed him to a shop in the most worn section of town. An old man crouched inside what was little more than a hole in the city wall. It was filled with dented lamps, faded rugs, and cracked pottery—a jumble of this and that.

"A fine spot I've leased to you," said Gindar.

The old man didn't answer.

"Your rent payment is due, Zaki. But the property is more valuable now, so I am forced to double the amount."

Zaki held out a leather pouch.

Gindar took it, counting the coins. "As I said, I must have twice this. If not . . ." He shrugged, as if helpless.

The old man spoke at last, his voice like the prying of a rusty nail. "Take this instead. It is of great value."

An ugly sound grated in Gindar's throat, and he spat into the street. "You have nothing—"

His eye caught the sparkle of gold, and he reached for the small box in Zaki's hand. It was encrusted with rubies and pearls, the craftsmanship beyond anything Aminah had ever seen.

"Where did you find such a thing?" asked Gindar.

"No matter," said Zaki. "Take it, but listen to me first. Do not open the box, or it will bring you grief. Sell this bit of gold as fast as you can, taking the profit to pay my debt."

"Agreed," said Gindar. He hurried from the shop before Zaki could change his mind.

Aminah wondered why the old man hadn't sold the box himself. It was worth more than he owed. Then she heard Zaki mutter, "Now Gindar will pay *his* debt."

She hurried after Gindar and found him in the dark recess of a narrow alley. He fondled the golden box and tried to lift the lid. When he couldn't open it, he felt for a hidden latch. "Something of greater value is inside," he muttered to himself.

Gindar pulled a knife from beneath his jubba and pried. The box lid flew open, and he screamed. Purple light flashed in his face, and his features began to melt. He dissolved into a lavender mist and was sucked into the box with the force of a hurricane. The lid snapped shut.

Aminah heard a shuffling step enter the alley. Zaki stooped and picked up the box, now ordinary brass studded with bits of colored glass. He smiled and hobbled back to his shop.

She followed and crouched in the shadow of an alley, watching the old man sort through his collection of tarnished brass lamps. Finally choosing one, he rubbed a finger across the spot where Aminah knew a tiny star was engraved. Then Zaki reached for the box and held it close to the lamp.

"Your new home, Gindar," he said.

)

AMINAH PRIED HER MIND from the orb and collapsed onto her bed. She awoke the next morning with a dull ache behind her eyes. Squinting in the sunlight that streamed into her room, she scratched at the mild rash that covered her body. As she reached for Barra's salve, Gindar's hard features jumped into Aminah's thoughts, and she began to cry.

Later, Idris and Barra noticed her swollen eyes and begged her to tell them what was wrong, but she wouldn't reveal Jinni's secret. Assuming she was pining for Hassan, Idris managed an indulgent, if not melancholy, smile.

The pain behind her eyes eased with the downing of ample amounts of headache powder—eating helped her feel even better—and, by midmorning, she was ready to face Jinni. She broke off from the solitary work of packing her belongings and called to him. To her surprise, he was actually helping Idris cart Barra's things to the stable.

Jinni was slow to follow Aminah into her quarters. Once inside, he looked into her eyes and said, "It is not pleasant, is it?"

Aminah shook her head, and then told him everything. She tried to soften the blow by saying, "At least you loved Jamila."

"As the saying goes, 'Even a hateful man can love his own mother.'" Jinni covered his face with his hands. "Or his own sister. Never call me Gindar. Never!"

"But you're a better person now," she said.

His laugh was bitter. "How can I be a better person? I am not even a man."

"But you've been kind to me. Leastways as of late."

"You are too forgiving, Miss."

Aminah covered his hand with hers, but he pulled away.

"I was all that I now despise in humans," he said. "Zaki did me a great favor."

"I've figured out how to help you, Jinni," said Aminah. "But I'd need my traveling powers back. I'm willing to ask Barra—she'd still have a wish left over to get us to Tyre. Then I'll go back in time to Al-Hirah and find Gindar before the box takes him—before he . . . you were made a demon. Somehow I'll stop him from opening that box."

"But it would change everything," he said. "We would never meet. You would still be starving on the streets of Al-Kal'as. So would Aladdin. And Idris. And what about Ahab?"

Aminah hadn't bargained for this. She struggled to find an answer. "It should be your choice," she said at last.

"Thank you," said Jinni. His bottom lip quivered. "I have not had a choice about my life since opening the golden box. I am grateful."

"Should I do this, then?" Her chest felt hollow.

Jinni drew in a tremendous breath and was slow in letting it out. "Even I am unsure your plan would work. If you were able to stop me from opening the box, then you would no longer have a jinni to grant traveling powers in the first place. Who knows what would happen. But it does not matter. I like myself better as a demon than a man such as Gindar. I see little hope that he would change, even with a second chance. No, Miss, I will stay with you and Barra."

Eleventh Moon

· Twenty-four ·

THE HOUSE SAT on the outskirts of Tyre. Its ample grounds and stables spread themselves across a hilltop overlooking the sea. Heavy walls surrounded the entire estate, giving its inhabitants a satisfying sense of security. A rumor spread through the city that the strange assortment of dwellers living there had come from Cyprus, and so Aminah and her family were the only ones to know that their smallest stable, looking out of place among the others, had traveled with them from Al-Kal'as.

When they'd first arrived in Tyre, Barra had insisted on using her last wish for the house. With the wish made, she'd wanted to toss the lamp to Aminah, but Aminah's hands had been clasped tightly in Hassan's.

Barra had commanded Jinni to raise the house slowly, to give the appearance that workmen were building it so that no one would suspect magic. He had had great fun creating the illusion of a vast workforce gathering on the hill, supplied by daily delivery wagons. Despite all his efforts, no one in the city had paid much attention. "Stupid humans," he'd complained, but Aminah had been pleased that people had asked few questions and rarely had come out to see what was happening.

Four wishing moons came and went before the house was completed. "A bit too fast for human construction," Jinni had said. "But money for staying in a kahn is running short. Why you gave the money box to Idris is beyond my understanding, Miss. And why one of you will not wish for more gold is even more difficult to fathom."

When at last they made the move from kahn to hilltop, there wasn't money left to furnish the house. Hassan's bakery made enough to feed them, but not much more, as most of his bread filled needy mouths. Still, Barra refused to wish upon the lamp, and Hassan only laughed when Aminah suggested he be the one.

"You'll have to take it back, Aminah," said Hassan. "Or perhaps you'd rather sleep on the floor."

"And have me cook meat on a stick," Barra said, "seeing as we have no pots—not even a knife."

"Why didn't we bring our pots?" Aminah grumbled. "There was room in the stable for them—and for all the beds."

"Good question, to be sure," said Barra, "but we didn't, so now you need to make a wish or two."

Aminah turned to Hassan for support, but he shrugged and said, "He's really your jinni. That's clear to both of us. But know that I'm willing to sleep on the floor. It might be a safer undertaking than getting caught up with a demon again."

Aminah nodded but still allowed Barra to take her hands and cup them around the lamp. Then Barra and Hassan stood staring at her until she cried, "All right! I'll rub the thing!"

Jinni sprang from the lamp. "Hello, hello!" he called out. "Marvelous to be back in your employ, Miss."

"Look at him," Hassan whispered to Barra. "The demon's got a grin that wraps around his head and touches in the back."

"He's so jubilant he's forgotten his usual roaring and thundering about," said Barra, and then she smiled. "Though I think it's quite dashing when he does."

Hassan's look was puzzled. "You sound as if . . ."

"Perhaps I do," she said.

"Well, if demons can be happy, this one certainly is," said Hassan. "But I'm still not certain I trust him."

Jinni bowed, not once but three times. "I am the thrall of whoso hath the lamp. Ask whatsoever, my lady, and it shall be thus."

"Jinni, as the old saying goes, 'Money is salve,'" said Aminah, trying her best to look severe. "So ease our discomfort. Give me a box that will always replenish its gold, just as before."

"Hearkening and obeying!" Jinni snapped his fingers, and a small chest appeared. It rattled and trembled as the coins roiled and tossed like an angry sea, rising so rapidly that they spilled over the edge.

"Thank you," said Aminah. "Are we back to the 'whosoes' and 'whatsoevers'? It's not necessary, you know."

"It helps me remember who I am," he replied. "I think that is best, do you not agree?"

Aminah nodded.

"For better or for worse, Jinni and his true mistress are reunited. So I suppose this calls for a celebration," said Hassan. He whipped the cloth from a tray he'd carried into the room without anyone's noticing. "My newest creation. I call them cream puffs."

☽

LATER, WHEN HASSAN RETURNED to the bakery, Aminah called Jinni from the lamp once again. He seemed hesitant as he stepped out of the brilliant cloud that billowed from the spout.

"I am here to please," he said, bowing.

"I've never seen such bright color," said Aminah, gesturing toward bars of purple light flashing on the surface of a cloud.

"Neon," said Jinni. "New York City was once a rainbow of neon."

"Amazing! You'll have to tell me all about it sometime. As well as Australia and Elvis Presley."

"Of course, Miss."

Aminah stepped forward and grasped his hand. His skin was cold, as if indeed no heart beat in his breast. "Jinni, we're back together, but things aren't the same. You can't be my Uncle Omar anymore."

"No, I cannot," he said.

"But I think we can still be friends, even without pretending you're something other than a demon. Don't you think so?"

Jinni smiled.

"Good. Now that's settled, I'd like to use my last two wishes. It's time to get back to work helping people like Ahab, and so I need my traveling powers back. I'd like to visit Idris, too, and I want to introduce myself to Talib and Nazreen. May I have them?"

Jinni crossed his arms. "So be it," he said.

Aminah felt the telltale tickle behind her breastbone. She drew in a deep breath and smiled. "As for my third wish, I'd like to have back the orb. I didn't really think you'd return it to the wizard."

"It seemed the safest thing to do," said Jinni. "But I told him you might need to use it again sometime." He snapped his fingers, and the crystal sphere appeared, once again cradled in its golden cup.

"Thank you," said Aminah, reaching out to touch her old friend. The orb winked a ruby-red greeting. "Would you like a game of chess, Jinni?"

"It is about time," said Jinni. "I have missed beating you."

The game lasted two hours before Jinni won.

"I think you cheat," said Aminah. "I suppose a jinni has lots of ways to cheat a mere human."

"Perhaps we should try backgammon," he said. "It relies more on luck than skill. You might have a better chance."

"You've done it now," she said, laughing. "I'm angry, and I always win when I'm angry. Wait until tomorrow; you'll see."

As Jinni put away the chess pieces, Aminah crossed to the window and peered through the carved wooden shutters. The moon was growing fat again, its blue light silhouetting palm fronds and cypress branches that swayed gently in the night breeze.

She turned back to Jinni and said, "Finish up the food and drink. I'll be back in a moment." The demon descended on the trays of fruit and pastries, hardly noticing she'd left the room.

When Aminah returned from her sleeping chamber, she found Jinni drinking straight from a pitcher of lemon sherbet. She laughed at his dripping beard, and he grinned at her, unapologetic.

"It's almost time, you know," Aminah said as Jinni wiped his mouth on his sleeve. "I'm going to need all three wishes."

"I believe you have been using the orb," said Jinni. "And you have already found someone. Am I right?"

She nodded. "In the future. Her name is Ella, and she lives in France. Do you know France, Jinni?"

He raised his eyebrows. "This Ella, would she have a stepmother? And two stepsisters? A beastly threesome, as I remember."

Aminah turned in surprise. "You know her?"

Jinni grinned. "So, you are the one."

"'The one'?"

"Yes, the one," he said. "Somebody has to do it, and it seems you have been chosen. I think we are perfect for the job. By the way, you are right about Ella. She will do a great deal of good in the world."

Aminah sighed. "You're speaking in riddles again. What job?"

"Fairy godmother," said Jinni.